I0598223

Transient Singularity

Eric D Tokajer

MDN
P.O. Box 10943
Pensacola, Florida 32524

Transient Singularity
ISBN
978-0-9894901-5-3

Published by:
MDN
P.O. Box 10943
Pensacola, Florida, 32524

Front cover design by:
Jeremie Webb

For my wife, Pammy, who for 33 years has not only endured my creative endeavors but has encouraged them.

Preface

Every event in life no matter how wonderful or tragic is completely dependent upon many smaller events. An adjustment of a single seemingly insignificant event can change the entire course of history. Armed with that knowledge Senator James Madison forms a secret government agency with the resources and ability to manipulate those minute moments in time.

Table of Contents

Preface.. 4

Chapter 1.. 8

Chapter 2.. 12

Chapter 3.. 15

Chapter 4.. 19

Chapter 5.. 22

Chapter 6.. 25

Chapter 7.. 28

Chapter 8.. 31

Chapter 9.. 33

Chapter 10.. 36

Chapter 11.. 38

Chapter 12.. 41

Chapter 13.. 43

Chapter 14.. 46

Chapter 15.. 49

Chapter 16.. 52

Chapter 17.. 55

Chapter 18.. 59

Chapter 19.. 62

Chapter 20.. 65

Chapter 21.. 69

Chapter 22.. 73

Chapter 23 77

Chapter 24 82

Chapter 25 86

Chapter 26 90

Chapter 27 95

Chapter 28 99

Chapter 29 105

Chapter 30 108

Chapter 31 111

Chapter 32 115

Chapter 33 119

Chapter 34 123

Chapter 35 126

Chapter 36 130

Chapter 37 134

Chapter 38 138

Chapter 39 142

Chapter 40 146

Chapter 41 151

Chapter 42 155

Chapter 43 159

Chapter 44 162

Chapter 45 166

Chapter 46 171

Chapter 47 175

Chapter 48 178

Chapter 49 182

Chapter 50 186

Chapter 51 190

Chapter 52 193

Chapter 53 197

Chapter 54 201

Chapter 55 206

Chapter 56 210

About the Author 212

Chapter 1

Closets, small spaces filled with every item one can imagine. You would think one would have gotten used to them after a few years of spending so much time hidden behind their walls. As Thomas stood, pressed against the side of his latest closet leaning against the corner, just out of view of the slatted doors, he thought about how many interesting and different types of doors he had seen on closets. He marveled at the amount of time and money spent by some homeowner to choose just the right door for a closet, only to fill the space with all of the junk that they did not want anyone else to see. There is a reason people refer to problems in one's past as "skeletons in the closet."

For Thomas, the thought of going into another closet was personally painful--not because of the claustrophobia or the sizes or volumes that were stashed in a closet, but because of his childhood experience of having been sent to the closet as a form of punishment. He still thought of closets as kiddie prison, and he had to come to terms with those memories every time he had to stand hidden within the sanctuary of a closet while patiently waiting for the perfect time to exit. As he continued to stand as still as humanly possible, his thoughts turned to his time within the real penal system first as a teenager. Like the junk strewn into the back of the closet, Thomas felt as if prisons were the closets of society, where all those people that no one wanted to be visible were tossed until such a time as they were needed again.

Thomas looked one more time at his wristwatch to see how long it would be until he could quietly step out of his hiding place and make his way home again. Home: a very simple apartment with simple furniture and just enough decorations to make it nondescript. As a matter of fact, the one word that would best describe everything about Thomas was "nondescript." It was one of the two main qualifications that allowed him to be chosen.

In any crowd at any time, Thomas was the one person no one seemed to notice was present. He was the man that nothing about him drew any attention--not his hair, not his clothing, not his manner. He just naturally seemed invisible. Not invisible like a chameleon that blends into the environment, but rather so average that even though everyone sees him clearly, no one seems to ever remember that he was around.

This uniqueness of being un-remember-able was something he learned early in life. As the fourth of six children and the third of four boys, he learned to blend quietly into the crowd among his siblings. By the time he went to school he could come and go in his classroom without his teachers even noticing. By the time he entered middle school, where students change rooms, he often stayed in class through attendance and quietly left unnoticed by students or teachers. By high school he mastered the ability to get high grades and perfect attendance while only spending a few minutes in class each day.

It was in the middle of high school that Thomas learned how profitable not being noticed could be. He came to realize that due to people never seeming to pay attention to his presence he could enter stores and leave with everything from bubble gum to jewelry without anyone even questioning his actions. He was more like a shadow in peoples' minds than a person. His prowess as a thief allowed him to leave home and rent his own apartment and ultimately the home he now lived in.

At the age of 26 Thomas had achieved much more than many other young people his age. He now lived in a nicely kept cookie-cutter home in an upper middle class neighborhood. He drove a late model, mid-sized imported car, which he kept clean and well maintained but was not something that would stand out to anyone watching traffic drive by. Even though he had been successful thus far, he understood his success was predominantly because he didn't stand out; therefore, his home, like his car and his clothing, was chosen so that no one would pay attention to it at all.

As a matter of fact, it was his NOT standing out from the crowd that finally drew attention to him by those whom he was working for, and ultimately was the reason he was standing in a closet today.

Chapter 2

The soft leather overstuffed chair was comfortable and designed to go with the very large, very expensive solid wood conference table. The tables and chairs as well as the balance of the furniture and decorations in the room were specifically chosen to set the tone of how important any meeting held within the confines of the room was. Each person sitting in the room looked as if he or she were molded or sculpted according to specifications to fit into a room just like this one. Each wore what was known as a power suit, complete with matching tie and handkerchief tucked precisely into the breast pocket. Along with their perfectly chosen and pressed garments, each had just the right amount of accouterments: an executive hairstyle; a simple gold wedding band to show moral commitment; a watch expensive enough to make a statement but not so expensive to appear opulent; and a class ring from a prestigious-name school recognized by all as elite. Those who were wearing glasses all wore this year's style, so no one could call them behind the times. Each attendee was sitting at just the perfect angle in his chair to denote an equal blend of interest and importance. Each individual did all he could to control the conversation and keep the focus on him. After all, they were chosen to represent their part of America and as such, would do everything within their control to see that their constituents were viewed as the highest priority in every discussion. That is, of course, as long as meeting the voters' needs didn't diminish their benefits. Slightly behind each man at the table were seated their staff members, each looking like a puppy just glad to be in the room, waiting for their master to show them some kind of attention even if it was only a kick under the table or a glance of disapproval. Just being in this room at this level was considered such a privilege afforded so few that even the mention of your name placed you in the realm of the big leagues. After all, it was those who were willing to serve and survived, who eventually were chosen to fill seats at the table. As those seated spoke as if delivering an address equivalent to the Gettysburg Address or maybe MLK's "I Have a Dream" speech, the staffers gallantly attempted to keep accurate notes while communicating bullet points to their respective gladiator in the battle for budget dollars and the pork projects that were part of the process. Each item was quid-pro-quo-- millions were spent just to get everyone to agree to spend thousands on whatever "real need" was brought to the table. In order to repair a bridge in Maryland, a road had to be fixed in Ohio, a park had to be remodeled in Kentucky and a beachfront dune project had to be approved in California. Each item required a majority agreement and each majority required a sizable amount of equality.

Chapter 3

Nothing compares to the feeling of sitting in a holding cell, wearing an orange jump suit, knowing that one is about to stand in front of a person who has within his power the ability to take away huge chunks of your life. Thomas had thought a lot about this day. You don't break the law the way he had and not think and even at times dream about this exact scenario. However, even in his worst nightmare he had not experienced the level of dread that he had in the last 24 hours. He was caught red-handed, as they say, leaving an auction house in preparations for its largest art and jewelry auction ever. This unusual sale resulted from the death of James Duncan a friend of Old Time Auction house owner Oliver Jamison, because James stipulated that his art and jewels be auctioned to the highest bidder at the business of his longtime friend. James, who made his fortune in the machining of small parts for military equipment, grew up with Oliver and made a running joke that with a name so formal sounding as "Oliver Jamison," running estate auctions was bound to be his fate. Oliver had done well over the years, providing his services to families whose loved ones passed away, leaving houses full of items that family members either had no room for or just plain didn't want for themselves. As the saying goes, one man's trash is another man's treasure. At 25% off the top, Oliver was more than happy to assist the bereaved with the dispersal of their loved ones' estate. This particular sale would be different, though. First, there were no heirs circling the sky waiting for the final payout. All proceeds after Oliver's fee would be going to charity. The other thing that made this sale unique was that everything being auctioned was desirable, with most items being wanted by more than one person. Every piece of furniture was an antique; each work of art was classic; and all of the jewelry was the kind found in high-end jewelry counters in big cities like New York. Because of the scope of the sale, the auction house was open the week before for people to preview all of the items so that they could decide which items they wanted to push for no matter what the cost versus which items were to be bid and won only if they could be bought at discount.

During this inspection period Thomas had entered and exited the building over and over without drawing notice from either the patrons or the top-notch security guards. He was not only able to help himself to a wonderful assortment of jewels but also to secure several small but beautiful and valuable pieces of sculpture. He had completed his "shopping" and was clear of the building and security, and had made his way down the road several miles when he saw a small child riding his tricycle into the road directly into oncoming traffic. Without thinking Thomas drove his Honda in front of the oncoming car, and thus kept the child from becoming the first traffic fatality of the year in that nice little hamlet. The problem was that in his entire adult life this was the first time Thomas had done anything to make himself stand out, or that was noticeable by anyone watching. Instead of being an unseen shadow he was suddenly a front-and-center hero. Since his car was damaged and un-moveable, his only option at this point was to calmly stay and wait for the police to finish their investigation of the crash.

As Thomas assumed the role of a man who did "what anyone else would have done," he could not have done a better job deflecting the accolades and minimizing the congratulatory handshakes and backslapping. After all information had been collected, insurance cards shared and both drivers told they were not at fault in the accident, the unthinkable happened and for the second time in one day Thomas was noticed. This time it was because the trunk latch of his car popped open, free of the lock mechanism. For some unknown serendipitous reason, just as everyone was getting ready to leave, the trunk popped up like a jack-in-the-box and the flashing lights from the police car shined upon the jewelry, creating a light show that would have embarrassed a disco. Everything froze. Moments later, Thomas was handcuffed and sitting in the back of a police car.

Chapter 4

Senator James Madison of Virginia, no relation at all to the 4th president although he was not above trying to connect the two any chance he had, was serving his second term when he was approached by a small man who reminded him very much of every mad scientist from every science fiction movie he'd ever seen. His visitor was slightly built, his small round glasses worn low on his nose caused him to bend his head way back just to look at someone who was standing at the same height that he was, which was just short of five feet. When Senator Madison looked up from his office desk he was surprised, not just by his short stature, but also by his disarray. It was rare in Washington for anyone to attend a meeting of any kind without first making sure he had prepared his outward appearance to impress the person or persons he was meeting with. It was not unusual for a lobbyist to change clothes ten times a day--once for each meeting-- so that each person was greeted by someone who had researched and knew his or her favorite color, styles, ball teams; really anything to have some kind of advantage in the first impression. After all, one only gets one chance to make a good first impression. In a city where impressions and appearances are currency and capital, to see someone in one's office who has clearly made an attempt at all to impress was, well, impressive.

Impressive was not a word that would used to describe Dr. Matthew Reading, a brilliant man who had spent most of his adult life working for NASA. A top Ivy League graduate, he was courted by universities and think-tank programs around the country but chose to work at NASA. This was not because of a love for space exploration, but because at the time NASA had a large budget and was being promoted as THE place where research and innovation were both encouraged and financed. As a young man, Matthew had an idea he was convinced would change the world. What he lacked was money to study, invent and produce his vision. He'd been at NASA more than 25 years and a new president had taken office and cut the budget of NASA to the bone. Thus, Dr. Reading's program was cut. It took some time and energy and a lot of promises, but in time private funding was found and the project had been completed to where a working model had been generated, and the next step was to put it into action. It was this next part which required the help of the Senator, who as chairman of the Senate Committee on Commerce, Science, and Transportation, had come into the office this morning. With a quick introduction by the chief of staff Bob Simon, without whose recommendation this meeting would have never happened, Matthew began to explain his invention, its uses and the importance of funding to make it available for use in the USA. For the first time in a long time the senator felt excited because of what could be accomplished by this simple yet amazing invention. In his mind he had committed to finding a way to make this happen, but outwardly he simply thanked the Doctor for coming while telling him he would present his project to the committee and do what he could to secure funding. He closed with the standard line "I am not making any promises."

Chapter 5

The day for Thomas had begun at 4:00 a.m. when the guards woke him and told him to get ready for arraignment. He knew what that was from talking to the guards and the growing number in lockup with him since he was processed in the evening before. He was simply to stand before the judge and respectfully answer one question: how do you plead?

There were three acceptable answers and only three: guilty, not guilty and no contest. After speaking and listening to everyone else in the cell, he decided he would plead not guilty. Not because he wasn't guilty, but because those with experience told him that a not-guilty plea would allow him to get a lawyer and hopefully arrange a plea bargain to reduce his sentence. It was a given he was going to prison; the only question at this point was for how long. By 5:30 they were all fed and started the journey to the courthouse. This began with the guards gathering all the men together and applying handcuffs and leg irons. These leg irons not only connected your legs together but also connected you to the man in front of you and behind you. Eventually the whole group looked very much like a millipede as each person walked in cadence together: right leg, left leg, right leg, left leg. Any variation of step would cause the ankle cuffs to pull and inflict pain to all affected. It didn't take long for everyone to get in step because in jail you don't want to give anyone a reason to be angry with you.

After rushing to get everyone ready to go, the wait for the prison van began. After only 30 minutes of waiting, described by some frequent flyers as record time, the prisoners and Thomas were loaded into the van and the drive to the courthouse commenced. This ride could best be described as torturous as the van was fitted with only hard plastic benches. Between the lurching, shuddering and shaking of the driver, who seemed dead-set against staying in any one lane for more than 30 seconds, the drive was more like slalom than a road course. The only break in the lurching was when the driver went out of his way to hit every pothole in the road, sometimes even slowing down to correct the course so as not to miss one.

At 7:00 the electric security door to the basement of

the courthouse opened with a loud creaking and the van pulled inside. The prisoners were all escorted to a holding room. Just before entering the stark room empty except for a single bench against the wall, the prisoners' leg shackles and handcuffs were removed. Removed, because a lawyer somewhere prevailed in a case that stated that it is prejudicial for a prisoner to be brought into court in handcuffs and leg shackles because it might make them look guilty to those who will be judging them.

Chapter 6

Senator Madison didn't let the day pass before he called a meeting with his upper staff to brainstorm about how to formulate a plan to make full and complete use of Matthew's invention. He knew it would take careful planning to put together a team that could not only make this happen but do so in a way that would keep the entire project a secret from all but the President and senior staff. Madison knew that if he could position himself correctly in this, he would become one of the most powerful men in not just the country but also the world. At first he even considered not bringing the president into the circle, but after some thought decided he would need his signature on any legislation which would be next to impossible without his being read in completely to the project and the process. After four days of almost 24-hour sessions, a plan was formulated to achieve the full funding of the program while still keeping it a secret. This is not really a new a thing in Washington, as many programs are fully-funded with taxes raised under the auspices of other programs. The old saying, " it is all in the fine print," is why in Washington it takes

500 pages to purchase an ink pen. The benefit of chairing the committee on Commerce, Science, and Transportation is that there is almost no limit to the items that can fall into one or more of those categories. With that in mind, slipping funding in for projects within projects is almost too easy. In this case it was determined that funding for the program would be directed through programs formed under the heading of commerce and science. Because the project was comprised of research and development it would be funded first through science; however, everyone knows that in science more is being diverted to green energy projects so the major funding would have to come through commerce. The idea was floated to levy a tax on all long distance phone lines. The provided intent would be to make sure that emergency phone lines would be available to everyone. Once established, some of those funds could be reapplied to this project. Those appropriations would later be worked into the official funding proposal under the covering of Television and Internet Services in Rural Communities to preserve equity in education for all citizens. The result of the meeting became The Universal Service Fund (USF) and its stated purpose was written as follows:

The United States Federal Communications Commission (FCC) created the Universal Service Fund in 1997 to meet Congressional universal service goals as mandated by the Telecommunications Act of 1996. The 1996 Act states that all providers of telecommunication services should contribute to federal universal service in some equitable and nondiscriminatory manner; there should be specific, predictable, and sufficient Federal and State mechanisms to preserve and advance universal service; all schools, classrooms, health care providers, and libraries should, generally, have access to advanced telecommunication services; and finally, that the Federal-State Joint Board and the FCC should determine those other principles that, consistent with the 1996 Act, are necessary to protect the public interest. With the passing of this legislation the project officially became government funded.

Chapter 7

For almost two full hours Thomas and his new friends sat in the holding room waiting for His Honor the judge to arrive and court to begin, each man doing his level best to act as if he feared nothing, speaking of either his total innocence, or of his plan to get a good lawyer to fight the system. While every man there was convincingly speaking his case and how he expected it to turn out, each also alternately complained about the justice system while sharing horror stories about friends or family members who were unjustly wronged by the system. Finally the heavy door opened and a guard called the first prisoner into the courtroom. One by one those in confinement were called without apparent rhyme or reason for the order called. Each one left for a short time and returned to share the results of his arraignment. Some were held over for trial and provided with court-appointed attorneys known as public defenders but often referred to as public offenders for their track record, due mostly to being overworked and underpaid. When you have limited time and limited resources you are limited in what you can do for a client. Others chose to plead guilty or no contest, which are essentially the same thing.

A guilty plea means you did it and no contest means you claim you did not, but don't want to fight about it. Both pleas result in immediate judgment and for those with misdemeanor charges after processing, most went home with either fines or probation. A few of those who pled out were given time in county jail with the longest sentencing being just less than one year. After half the men had their chance to stand before the judge, the guard came to the door and called Thomas' name. Thomas was amazed at all the thoughts that went through his mind in such a short walk. Fear of prison became very real; after all, he was charged with felony counts that could all result in prison time. But it wasn't only fear that gripped him. He was also curious as to what the judge would say, how he himself would respond, what the outcome would be, and if he ought to ask for a public defender or hire his own, and how much would that cost? All of these questions and more raced through his mind. The walk was only about 100 yards total but he had never talked to himself so much in such a short time. When he walked into the courtroom his head hurt from all the thinking. One thing he knew for sure was that he had never in his life felt so totally noticed and spot lit as when he stood in front of that huge desk and looked up at the man in the black robe. The judge began to explain the procedure; he reminded him that he was not there to try the case or present evidence but was only there to hear the charges against him and his plea. The judge went on to question if he understood all of the charges against him and if he understood his plea options. After Thomas replied that he did, in fact, understand both the charges and the available pleas, the judge asked the question Thomas had been waiting to hear for almost 24 hours. "How do you plead?" Before Thomas could answer, a door behind the judge opened and a woman walked up to the judge, apologized for interrupting, and whispered something into the judge's ear. The judge listened, looked perplexed for a moment and then, with a tap of his gavel, announced a recess. Thomas could not decide if he should be relieved or angered by the interruption.

Chapter 8

Passing legislation through both houses of Congress and getting a president to sign it was the easy part. The funding for development was now flowing and work on one end of the project had begun. Senator Madison was amazed how much work people were willing to do without knowing what it was they were actually doing or making. If you provide a nice salary, a good working environment and great government benefits, most people are willing to do what you ask of them. Of course, those who did ask questions were given prepared answers and those who refused to stop asking questions found themselves unemployed. Now Madison had to convince private corporations to cooperate in the project while providing them limited information beyond what was needed to complete the project and acquire a fully functioning system operational throughout the world. The worst part of negotiations was not what he had to say or do but whom he had to convince. All of the non-governmental participants would need to be from the entertainment industry: people willing to give away other people's money to save the world but very thrifty when their money was on the table. In order for this project to work, a conglomerate of television, Internet and cable companies would have to be formed. In the process networks would have to be pitched and formed that may on paper show little-to-no profit. These companies would, of course, benefit financially through backdoor funding through the new USF taxes and further revenue provided by future tax and fee programs. Madison knew the only way to make this happen would be to convince the companies that their participation would yield a financial windfall if they decided to play ball with the government on the project. If they chose not to join in as partners, the government would be forced for national security reasons to take over parts of their enterprises without their help and without benefit to them. It is shocking how generous and helpful people can be when they realize that they have no real option available other than to agree to help.

Chapter 9

Judge Robert Collins was one of those rare individuals who had achieved a level of success within the criminal justice system without compromising his values in the process. He was born in and stilled lived in the same city. He went to public schools and excelled in both academics and sports. His parents were still married and had just celebrated their 40th anniversary. His two brothers and one sister had all earned degrees and were successful in their professions, but he was the only one that had chosen public service. As a man of strong faith he had early in his life decided he would not use any of the available excuses for personal failures. He believed that honest hard work and dedication to personal and professional commitments were the secrets to success and he did everything he could to share that secret with everyone who would listen. After graduating from law school he married his wife Amanda, and together they were raising their son Robert Jr. and daughter Catherine just two blocks from the house he grew up in. He would never have considered living anywhere else. Robert Collins was the type of judge that every honest person was glad to have sitting on the bench, who every criminal understood would be fair and consistent in the decisions he handed down. This was very fortunate for Senator Madison who needed someone who possessed strong principles and commitment at this very moment.

After walking out the back door of his courtroom Judge Collins walked through the private hallways past the clerks offices and directly through the hardwood door with the glass insert with his name etched in beautiful calligraphy. He still felt a great sense of accomplishment and personal pride each time he saw his name with the title *Circuit Judge* so neatly written under it. He sincerely hoped he never lost that feeling.

As he walked into his office he saw three men standing there. Two he didn't recognize at all, but the third he had seen who knows how many thousands of times on TV and in the news. Here he stood looking face to face with the senior senator from his state. Senator Madison held out his hand to shake and the judge was impressed by the firm grip that made one feel as if the senator was the one being honored by the greeting.

For a moment Judge Collins hesitated to sit down, wondering what the proper etiquette was when welcoming a senator into one's office. He then walked around his large but unassuming desk and invited his senator to sit down, all the while trying to decide who he was going to call first--his father or his wife--to share his excitement of having someone so important visiting not just in his city, but coming directly to his office. He realized he would have to tell Amanda first because, well, he did have to wake up with her every morning for the rest of his life and he wanted that first glance to continue to be into a face with a broad beautiful smile on it.

Chapter 10

Senator Madison prepared for his meeting with the small city judge the same way he prepared for every meeting he had been a part of since he began in politics. He researched the man he would be meeting with, both his public life and his private life. He learned everything he could about the man, his family, and his positions both politically and personally. He knew what school he went to, every job he had held, whom he had dated and to whom he owed favors.

In most cases that last part was the most valuable information because if you knew whom someone owed then you could manipulate their point of view. The problem in this case was that Judge Robert Collins didn't seem to owe anyone anything. He had not become a judge with the assistance of power brokers; instead, he really was the choice of the voting public. This information grieved and impressed the senator at the same time.

He met with his aides and chief of staff and ran scenarios of conversations over and over until he felt they had arrived at a series of statements that would guide the conversation and the judge to the same conclusion. He would appeal to the judge as a patriot and a family man who would want the best for his country and his family as well as families the world over.

When you find a man who will not compromise his values, your plan must be to present your need in a way that agrees with those values. He would give Judge Collins the opportunity to save the world that he had spent so much time trying to save. He was convinced that a man who had dedicated his life to serving others would jump at the chance to serve in a world-changing capacity.

He also knew that a man of such strong integrity and convictions would honor his word to keep the program absolutely confidential. The senator knew the only motivation stronger than the corrupt values of personal gratification are the sincere values of faith and service. He was prepared for his meeting with the Honorable Judge Robert Collins.

Chapter 11

Once Judge Collins got beyond the excitement of having a senator in his office the excitement changed to intrigue. Why was he there? What did he want? The different thoughts soared through his mind like competing meteor storms. He searched his mind for anything that he had done or been involved in that would require or deserve a visit from such a significant guest. For the life of him he could not come up with a reason for the visit and upon concluding that there was not reason he knew of, he entered back into real time and welcomed his guest to his hometown.

As they exchanged the requisite pleasantries about the wonder of life in a small city, Judge Collins wondered if the senator meant any of what he was saying, while at the same time knowing that small city life really was wonderful and pleasant.

After a sufficient amount of small talk, the Senator began to weave his prepared talking points into a conversation which he hoped would bring the judge both into agreement to help, and to do so in such a way that the judge felt it the right thing to do and not just expedient. This was important for the senator because if he could get him to feel it was the right thing to do, then he would not be in debt to the judge for any further reciprocal favors, knowing full well that favors are the currency of politics.

It took only moments for the senator to lay out his purpose for visiting and sharing the importance of making exceptions to the rule in order to accomplish the greater good. He shared a need for judicial discretion to be used in the case of Thomas Green, the young man that only a short time before had been standing before him in his courtroom. Madison explained that although he could not get into the specifics, the federal government was asking the judge to turn Green over to him and expunge all record and reference to his arrest and appearance before the court. He explained that while he would leave the final decision to the judge, he wanted him to know with assurance that there were national and international implications to his decision and that many lives were depending on his willingness to trust the senator in this matter. He also made it clear that beyond the knowledge of the importance the federal government had placed on this case and the subject involved, he was not there to offer anything beyond the thanks of the president and Congress for his assistance. Madison knew that with a man of character this last statement was really the icing to seal the deal. Men of integrity didn't trade favors; they responded based upon convictions and deep-seated commitment. The smallest hint of any "payoff" for help would have slammed the door and been the death knell to Thomas' participation in the program. This negotiation was a skillful game of chess and with one clear statement he had placed the judge in checkmate. After finishing the explanation in a very calm and quiet way, the senator asked Collins to consider it for a few minutes and make his decision, while knowing completely by the look in his eyes that Collins had already made his decision to help. When you provide a servant the opportunity to serve, they do what comes naturally to them.

Chapter 12

"All rise!" The clear loud voice of the court officer cried out as the judge returned to his seat. The judge apologized for the sudden interruption and asked the state attorney to recall the last defendant. A moment later Thomas was brought back into the courtroom, prepared once again to respond with his plea. Thomas stood quietly waiting on the judge to speak to him, resolved that he would be returning to the jail and ultimately spending time in a state prison.

To his surprise the judge leaned forward in his seat and announced that court would be recessing for lunch and all further arraignments would be handled after the break. Thomas again was confused -- why did the judge have him called, only to dismiss for lunch without even completing his arraignment? He thought to himself with only limited seriousness that this yo-yoing of his case may have been considered torture and even have met the criteria of cruel and unusual punishment.

On Thomas' way back to the holding cell for the

second time, the guard supervising his transportation stopped and turned into a conference room. Thomas knew immediately this was not a room normally used for prisoner conferences. It was far too well decorated with comfortable chairs and even plants and paintings.

Thomas was told to take a seat and that a lawyer had been assigned to his case and would be in shortly to discuss it and assist in his defense. Mixed feelings would be considered the understatement of the day. Up, down, in, out, right, left -- it seemed as if the longer the day went the more interruptions and changes took place. Whoever the public defender was, Thomas decided that he was going to inform him that he planned to hire his own lawyer, and that while he appreciated his willingness to help he wanted someone with more time and resources on his side during trial.

Chapter 13

When Senator Madison stepped into the room he could tell immediately that Thomas had no idea who he was, a sad commentary on the failure of schools to instruct students on government as part of social studies. However, this was not the time to start a diatribe about the failures of the public education system. He had only a few minutes to make his case to Mr. Green and convince him that he should "volunteer" his services to the government of the United States of America. In exchange for his commitment to serve he would receive complete absolution for all crimes committed previous to the time of entering service.

This would be one of the most unusual meetings he had ever been involved in due to the unique dynamics of the participants compared to his "typical" meetings. Any man in politics would immediately notice the difference in attitudes of one who recognized a man of position from one who did not. One who was in the know always tried to demonstrate the proper level of respect and admiration necessary to acquire whatever it was he was seeking, while at the same time trying to retain whatever self-respect he had. He would do all this while knowing that at some level he was standing hat in hand before someone he at least believed could provide what he was in essence begging for at any given time.

The balance of these goals was often just beyond the reach of the average person, who would either appear to go too far in adulation to the point of groupie status, or would come off too proud to lower himself to the level of subjugation he felt was required to achieve his goal.

This time things were different. This time it was he who had entered the room with hope of receiving something. His goal was to get what he desperately needed without appearing desperate while convincing the young man across the table that he was doing him a favor by providing a means of escape from the legal problems he faced.

He had been in thousands of similar meetings with lobbyists who had mastered the fine art of the spin. In the hands of a spin expert, every situation, no matter how desperate, could be turned into a profitable opportunity. Spin experts could somehow make a natural disaster look like an investment opportunity; a business failure look like a growth opportunity and a war look like an economic boom.

It was these professional spinners who had convinced Americans that crime was the fault of environment; that divorce was not really destruction of families, that asking people to prove eligibility for benefits was really veiled racism.

It was because of his lengthy experience with these modern-day snake oil salesmen that he felt comfortable in what he was about to try even though he was totally out of his comfort zone trying it.

Chapter 14

Thomas looked at the gentlemen who sat down so smoothly into the chair opposite him and thought two things: first, that "gentleman" was an often-overused word but this man would have made a good photo to put next to the word in the dictionary. Second, he realized that this man was not a public defender.

His suit and tie were expensive, the kind of material that you almost felt compelled to reach out and touch just to see how it felt. He had a Rolex watch that Thomas recognized instantly from having taken so many of them from houses that he had "shopped." Not one hair was out of place and his hands looked as if he had never done a real day's work in his life. It occurred to him that this man was exactly the type of man that he would have targeted.

The whole matter of sizing the stranger up took less than 20 seconds, but even with the information gleaned by this quick once-over Thomas was still as perplexed as he was when he was first let into the conference room. Who was this man and what did he want?

Then suddenly he had heard himself thinking out loud. As if time stood still, he realized that his thoughts had changed from, "What can he do to help me?" to "What does he want?" Thomas instantly sensed a change in the winds of fortune. This man had the look of someone who wanted something from him and wanted it badly.

Thomas made a mental accounting, trying to think of anything of value he had that this man could want. He was trying to go through the inventory of items he had acquired and not yet sold to a new collector. For the life of him, he could not think of anything valuable enough for a man of this caliber to meet him personally. If he were just after the normal ill-gotten spoils of his profession, then why would he not go through regular channels? After the hearings and trials all items recovered would be available for claim by their rightful owners. So Thomas concluded if it was about recovering stolen property, it was not about recovering something that this man had legal claim to, or it was something that he didn't want being made public for one reason or another.

This did, however, prepare Thomas for what would come next: the negotiation, the give and take, the process of trying to get as much as one could while only giving as little as possible. This was something he was both familiar with and good at. Any thief that had found a level of success in the business learned how to negotiate for things of value. The only question now was what this stranger wanted and was Thomas' freedom equal in value to the item. He was suddenly and unexpectedly hopeful.

Chapter 15

James Madison sat down at the table and with one
smooth move, laid his briefcase down and opened it
up. He pulled out an official-looking, half-inch thick
file folder with two words on top in bold print:
Thomas Green. Madison placed the briefcase on the
chair next to him and opened the file in such a way
that Thomas could see what was inside. This tactic
was used to make Thomas comfortable, that nothing
was being hidden but everything was out in the open
while Madison was still was in control of what was
being shown. In the file were a series of legal
documents, arrest reports, photographs and witness
statements. Behind them was a document with a
title Thomas was familiar with but he had never
actually seen: a letter of amnesty. Behind those
documents in a pile not fully visible was what
seemed to be a report of the life and times of
Thomas Green. This report superficially showed an
unremarkable life, yet it was the very reason that
Madison was sitting at this table after driving all
night just to get here in time to make this meeting
happen.

The senator placed the three sections of papers into three different piles and then began to follow through on the plan that was established with his staff back in Washington. Every step, every word, and every movement had been discussed and decided upon in order to achieve the desired result. Just as a salesman is taught to ask as many questions as possible to elicit a yes response from the customer, his team had designed a script to direct the conversation to its only logical conclusion, or at least the logical conclusion that the senator wanted Thomas to come to.

He began by introducing himself and letting Thomas know that he was not there as a senator, but as a representative of a collective of people interested in helping people like Thomas get themselves out of the problems they had gotten themselves into. This group searched for people who had talents and abilities but were using them in a way contrary to the expectations of a productive and peaceful society. They looked for people like Thomas who would have become productive members of society but because of the course of their lives had chosen to travel the wrong path. This path had brought him to where he was today, where he was suddenly being extended a one-time offer to turn his life around and become a giver instead of a taker. As the conversation progressed Madison went through all of the documents related to Thomas' case, moving quickly but careful not to omit any details which would make it look as if he didn't understand just how much trouble Thomas was in. He added details on just how long Thomas could expect to be incarcerated if it weren't for the benevolence of the people he represented.

Chapter 16

Dr. Matthew Reading, the eminent physics professor, looked down at the face of his 5-year old son and experienced the same unbelievable feeling of amazement he'd had so many times before, a feeling he was certain was universal to every parent the world over, no matter what culture or faith background one held to: the amazement that somehow, in some way, he was involved in bringing life into this world. From the first time he looked at his son in the hospital until this very moment--even with his background in science--life still amazed him. The more he studied and the more he understood the complexities of the universe, the more he knew that he would never be able to comprehend the vastness of it all.

Today was Wednesday, his day to spend time with his son. One of the non-negotiable items in his contract with the university was that he would have Wednesdays off for family time. The university quickly agreed, and would have without hesitation allowed him more than just one day if that's what it took to get him to join the staff. Just being able to add his name to the letterhead had increased the institution's status in the academic community. In addition, alumni donations had increased dramatically from the moment the contract had been signed.

So here he was, a man highly respected by academics the world over, sitting on the floor with his son watching "Willy Wonka and the Chocolate Factory" on television, though the reality was that he was much more involved in watching his son experience the excitement of the movie than he was actually watching the movie. Every sight and sound was brand-new to 5-year old Micah. The opening of the movie was a little slow for him, but once he got his first look at the candy factory, and all of the colors, the Oompa Loompas with their orange faces and the almost unimaginable chocolate river he was hooked. Matthew thought back to the first time he had watched this movie with his father and realized that memories were being made between a father and son that would be long-remembered: Violet chewing her gum until she turned into a giant blueberry; Augustus drinking from the chocolate river until he was sucked into the tube disappearing into the chocolate machine; spoiled little Veruca who was a bad egg; and last but not least, Mike, who was shrunk while being streamed through Wonkavision technology.

In between the songs, dances and rebellious activities of the ticket holders as they travelled exploring the factory, Dr. Matthew Reading discovered something that would change the world forever.

Chapter 17

Thomas felt the familiar vibration of the timer in his wristwatch warning him that he had five minutes to prepare to exit the closet. These last few minutes were always the worst to deal with, knowing that shortly he would be able to leave the confines of the closet and stretch his joints out with freedom of movement. It was also in these short moments that everything would run through his mind: everything that could go right and everything that could go wrong. What could go wrong? He could be seen; he could be caught; or even worse, he could be late, which would be catastrophic.

While most people his age seemed to think that being on time was inconsequential, Thomas knew too well what problems not being timely could cause. Only those people who have an extremely time-sensitive occupation realize just how long 60 seconds really is. For most people most of the time, time flies quickly. But everyone knows that it takes longer to drive to your vacation location than it does to drive home.

The human mind somehow relates differently to time when waiting on something and Thomas was definitely waiting. Looking at his watch he realized that he only had to wait four minutes and thirty seconds longer to break out of the closet and step out into the real world once again.

He looked down at his tennis shoes, which were simple and had just the right amount of wear and tear so that they looked broken in. He was wearing a plaid button-down shirt and Wrangler jeans. He had to think quickly--was his shirt supposed to be tucked or un-tucked? To Thomas it was the little things like that, which could keep him from accomplishing his task.

Shirt tucked or un-tucked doesn't seem like much but Thomas' whole life depended on knowing those little seemingly insignificant details. He finally remembered he needed to be un-tucked today, so moving slowly and quietly so that no one would hear him he un-tucked his shirt and looked at his watch again. Two minutes left. He listened for any movement within hearing distance and prepared to walk out into the office.

Once out he knew he only had 17 minutes to complete his objective and make his way safely to his next location. He had done this hundreds of times now, each time aware of how vital every step was and what was riding on his not just finishing the job, but doing so in such a way that no one would ever know he had been around. He paid close attention to every detail: making sure no footprints were left in carpet; no fingerprints left anywhere; and anything moved placed back exactly to its original position with the exception of the one item that Thomas was responsible to change. But even that had to be changed in such a way that no one would know the change took place.

Time was up. Thomas carefully slid the door open, walked out into the room lit only by the outdoor streetlights and stepped directly to the far side of the desk, the small desk in the corner where from first look everyone would assume the person who was least important worked. If everything went according to plan, the young lady who sat at that desk for eight hours every day would never know how important she really was.

Thomas pulled a pen from the glass canning jar on the desk, removed a list from a file folder marked "luncheon" and carefully rewrote the list alphabetically, adding one name to it. When finished the new list looked exactly as the old one had, other than the additional name. He placed the pen back in its location, replaced the page into the file folder and restored it to its place of the desk, and then carefully finally left the room and the building.

Chapter 18

 After getting the bill through Congress and signed by the president, Senator Madison scheduled a series of meetings with men of means who would finance the program without being questioned about their intentions. Madison knew that when people do things that appear crazy they become targets of investigative reporters and become punch lines on late-night television programs. That is, unless those people are the very wealthy, as billionaires rarely have their motives or sanity questioned. Why? Because those who would question them tend to work for them or in some way owe them a debt too big to take a chance on losing their support.

In these meetings Madison explained the need for a 24-hour cable television channel that would play old movies, old programs and even old commercials. It could also run advertisements from new products to build revenue but the station's primary support would be a new government program.

He would explain how the family values block in Congress raised such a fuss over the degrading programming on television that keeps eroding the family and family values that the members were going to start a censorship agency if the "liberal crowd" didn't do something to provide opportunities to present old-fashioned morals and values on TV again.

He knew that the men in this room, most of who made their riches from the production of programs that would be censored, would be willing to do whatever was needed to make this problem go away, especially since it was not going to cost them anything but would end up increasing their fortunes through government support of their new network.

So, with almost a wave of a wand, a brand-new network was born and would be added to every cable network throughout the country. The Passage of the Telecommunications Act of 1996 and the formation of this new network happening in the same year went unnoticed by the media and everyone else except Senator Madison and his team.

It amazed the senator how much one could do without anyone paying attention to it, if the right people were involved in making it happen. He had just structured a project that affected not only the entire government but also every state and city in the country with almost no media coverage of the new government program nor the connective branches of television, cable and media empires.

Chapter 19

Thomas weighed his options. On one hand, there was a lengthy prison sentence enclosed in a cell surrounded by other men who were always miserable and depressed with nothing to keep them busy except thinking about where they wish they were. On the other hand was full immunity and complete and total amnesty for all crimes committed up to and including the date of signature.

To an outsider, the decision would seem to be easy to make. The path of least resistance appeared clear: prison or freedom? However, he also knew that freedom wasn't really free. The real question pounding in his mind and causing his heart to race was what was the actual cost going to be?

But even with that thought running through his mind he also knew that no matter what the cost he was not going to choose spending most of his life in prison over immediate freedom. If whatever he was going to be asked to do was more than he was willing to do, he would just disappear--something he had plenty of experience in doing.

He leaned forward in his chair and with every effort to remain casual, posed the million-dollar question: "What is it exactly that you want from me?" Thomas knew that negotiations were and always would be wars to be fought on the battlefield of the bargaining table. He also knew that in most of his past negotiations he used the value of the items he was offering for leverage in the process. The more valuable, uncommon and desired items were, the better his negotiating position. Known as higher ground on a battlefield, this position was desired by both sides of the exchange.

Thomas knew they wanted him and considered him valuable because the offer on the table was a large opening salvo. What he didn't know was how rare they considered him. He had thought of starting the discussion with "why me?" which may have brought the conversation to a place where he would discover his rareness. Instead he decided to go with the straightforward approach and ask, "What did they want?" and "What is the cost?" This tactic could also produce a hint about how rare he was considered, but it would also let them know he understood their "gift" was not really a gift.

The other thing this question would prove was the trustworthiness of the man on the other side of the table. After all, it was clear that it would be he whom Thomas would owe, and owing someone you cannot trust is always a very dangerous position to be placed in.

He paid close attention to the way the senator would reply. Each word would be important. Not just the actual sounds emitted vocally, but also the expression, inflection and body language all would speak loudly, if one had the experience of listening with one's eyes.

Chapter 20

He thought to himself, "It was so simple!" How could
he be the first one to figure it out? Surely someone
else had come up with this idea before! As soon as
the movie ended he laid Micah down for his nap and
jumped on his computer. Turning it on, he heard
the almost comforting tune of the Microsoft start-up.
He logged on and opened a browser page, heading to
the place everyone went to when trying to find
something: the Internet. Typing in the URL for a
search engine, he typed keyword after keyword,
searching every possible combination of terms,
looking for even a glimpse of a website or journal
page that would include what he was looking for.
Amazed and bewildered, he was feeling the
exhilaration of invention while still guarding himself
for the immense letdown that would come if
someone else had, in fact, beat him to the punch.

Page after page opened up in front of him as the
screen glowed. As each site opened Matthew's
energy and excitement built up more as he
repeatedly filled in the search bar with the variant
keywords leading him from site to site. After three

hours of looking he finally started to relax a little and allow himself to believe that this thought, this idea, was his and his alone.

He continued his quest the rest of the day and into the night. He lost track of how many different sites and in how many different languages he had opened and closed some tabs more than once as he double and triple-checked his research. Correctly applied, this precision, although time consuming, would save hours and hours should he find out that someone else had previously come up with the same idea.

For the first time since his days in university Matthew woke up to the heat of the sun shining on his face while sitting in his desk chair. But this time something was different. With the heat of the sun came an internal reminder of why he was still in the chair. For a moment he just sat there enjoying the warmth and relaxing for the first time since the proverbial light bulb had gone off in his mind.

After all of his research, years of think-tank after think-tank, the solution to the question he had been working on came not through laboratory experiments but because he spent a couple hours watching a classic movie with his son.

Now that he was reasonably confident this idea had not been thought of previously, that it was completely untried, he sat down at his desk and started to map out a strategy to put his thoughts onto paper, which in actuality meant entering the information into his computer.

After a long deep breath he began. With the first few keystrokes, he realized he had not felt this kind of excitement about a project or idea in ages. This moment was why he entered science in the first place. For a moment he understood what great inventors like Edison, Bell and Marconi must have experienced when the inventions they created first came to them.

His mind spun with enthusiasm as the keys on his computer clicked away. He could not remember the last time he'd had such a steady stream of ideas flowing in such a way: thoughts free-falling through his mind, down his arms and directly to the keyboard.

Every single piece of a puzzle he had been trying to

put together for years suddenly and completely fell into place within his mind in what could only be understood as a revelation. What amazed him was that while it was happening it didn't seem to matter what part of the puzzle he was working on: he could see where every piece fit; how it connected to every other piece; and what each piece was to do.

He had never before experienced such a thing and could feel the exhilaration build as both his mind and pulse raced. He got to a point where the excitement was so strong that he feared continuing at such a pace, while simultaneously he feared stopping and somehow disconnecting from what seemed to be a computer download directly through him. He wondered if this was what a USB cable felt like.

Chapter 21

Senator Madison was equally interested in the body language and expressions of the young man seated across from him. He knew the young man was sizing him up, not only with his questions but also with his eyes. It was always interesting how these negotiations went; step by step, each side providing only a glimpse of information at a time while searching to receive as much information as possible in return. The offer on the table was significant yet even if Thomas accepted it, this was only phase one of the actual acceptance by Madison.

All of this effort could be for nothing if Thomas wasn't able to complete the entire battery of prepared tests in a way that demonstrated that he was, in fact, the right choice. Just accepting the offer made him eligible to continue through the induction program.

Madison and his team had worked through this process thoroughly to create an exam of sorts that would allow his team to test that Thomas intellectually, morally, physically, physiologically and psychologically would be able to fulfill every requirement for this new position. From their previous investigation Thomas met all prerequisites to this point.

Madison noticed that even when offered a complete pardon of all crimes, Thomas didn't rush to answer, but instead took time to both ask questions and even to challenge the senator in subtle ways, a very good start indeed.

Knowing that the answer to Thomas' first question would set the stage for all future questions and answers, Madison knew he had to be totally honest in his answer, while at the same time withholding information Thomas didn't need to know at this point.

Navigating this conversation required skill and thought; each question and answer had to be provided in such a way that the conversation would travel the desired path. Madison also knew that if it seemed he were thinking too long or too much it could be perceived as if he were trying to deceive versus just being careful. He would only have a few seconds between each question to consider all possible repercussions of each answer and what the next questions and answers might be as a result of what he was about to say.

With all of that in mind the senator leaned slightly forward and began to speak, his words carefully measured, spoken with just the right amount of seriousness, sincerity and touch of authority. He explained that a new agency was being formed and that they were looking for people with a special skill set that would be able to perform at a high level of secrecy. This new organization would involve people from almost every part of the government, and would have a large budget to accomplish its objectives. He told Thomas entry into the program involved many tests, both physical and mental, and that in order to be accepted into the program he would have to excel in each assessment.

He reiterated the extreme secrecy involved in the program and informed Thomas that if he chose to be involved he could not speak to anyone about the program, no matter what.

Finally Madison arose from his chair and told Thomas

he would give him ten minutes to decide what he wanted to do and then his decision would be required. He would only have one chance at this so he needed to think hard and long because it was a life-changer.

Before he left Thomas said he needed to know one thing before he could answer: what would happen to him and his legal issues if he did not complete or excel in the assessments? Would his pardon continue? Madison replied yes, once pardoned, his record would be gone even if he didn't complete the program. Madison was secretly pleased that Thomas was quick enough on his feet to make sure that no doors left open needed to be closed.

Chapter 22

Matthew Reading had accomplished more than he had ever dreamed of achieving. He not only came up with a theory that could significantly change history, he had also been able to acquire funding to bring his invention from theory to reality. Now he was standing in the outer office of one of the most powerful men in the country, the senior member of a senate committee, the one man who could help him to fund his invention from partly operable to fully functioning.

He realized the clock on the wall looked like it cost more than his current vehicle. The clock showed 17 minutes until his scheduled appointment. He began to think over where he started from and what he had been able to accomplish thus far. He had been able to both build a functioning machine and to test his machine on small inanimate objects. The next phase would be to experiment with living beings. This was beyond his current finances and way beyond any liability he was willing to assume. However, he understood that possible government involvement would both remove his personal liability and provide funding beyond anything he could find through his personal contacts. It was especially important that the confidentiality of the invention be kept at least until a patent could be acquired.

Matthew had come prepared to demonstrate his invention while reserving information on how the technology worked just in case things didn't go well and he'd have to search elsewhere for funding. He was not sure where exactly elsewhere was, but he hoped something as important as his machine would eventually be funded by someone.

As he stood in the outer office looking at the other people coming and going from the building, he immediately realized he was not dressed to the same level as they were. It never dawned on him to have put something more professional looking on; after all, he was a scientist and to him, a lab coat was professional. Now he started to hope that the senator would not judge a book by its cover and reject him out of hand simply because he was not dressed in a power suit. Was it even possible that the senator would consider his not dressing up for this meeting as a sign of disrespect and end the meeting before it even started?

Then he thought to himself that when he had spoken to the chief of staff to procure the meeting, the man never once mentioned an appropriate dress code or requirement of any kind. He looked at the clock again and saw he now had 15 minutes remaining till the meeting but for some reason he felt as if he had just concluded a marathon. Every fiber of his being seemed to be aching and sweating at the same time. He was not sure if he was cold or hot. He wanted desperately to sit down but was afraid he would not be able to summon the strength to stand up again if he did. All the way to the meeting he had convinced himself that he was not nervous but at this moment he was coming to the reality that not only was he nervous, he was nearly petrified. Not because of his invention, but because for the first time since the day he watched that movie with his son, he wondered if he was really the person who was supposed to figure all of this out. Was he worthy of being the inventor of this device? How in the world was this happening to him? And more importantly, would anyone take seriously a man who couldn't even think to put on a suit when meeting a senator? He looked at the clock one more time, realized he still had 12 minutes left, took a deep breath and saw the door open, and suddenly felt he needed those last 12 minutes really badly.

Chapter 23

Walking into the office one more day seemed like a trek across the desert. He had been working in the same office at this same desk for almost 18 years now and it felt as if he was no further along in his career path than when he graduated from university. For three and a half years in college he was at the top of his class. When he graduated with honors he expected that his life would continue down that same street of success, starting out with an entry-level job and working his way up the ladder to the proverbial corner office and all the perks that came with it. However, the corporate world was not the world of academia. He tried very hard to accomplish the tasks set before him, but somehow the fact that he was smart and hardworking didn't seem to rate as highly as those who were creative and assertive.

His job performance reviews were always good and he didn't fear losing his position. He had moved up a few rungs on the ladder but had never made the jump from worker ant to leader. Though his work was always cited as being well done and sometimes even exceptional, it was never in the same way that the many people who were promoted ahead of him were spoken of. Year after year he got a small increase when raises came but never the golden key to the executive suite he so longed for.

Each year around this time he would reevaluate his performance and consider looking for another place to work with opportunities he didn't see offered where he was. This time of year, the spring season, was when all the major promotions were made. The jump from drone to executive was always the highlight of the spring conference. Those who received an invitation to this conference were the lucky ones who had caught the eyes of someone somewhere with the gravitas to submit their names for advancement.

For 17 years he had looked in his mailbox for the "Golden Ticket," but year after year his box was empty. Year after year he watched others who were not as smart, not as thorough, not as dedicated, go to their boxes and open the gilded envelope slowly, as if they were going to announce the winner of this year's Oscars. Then the recipient would turn toward the audience and with feigned humility give his or her acceptance speech.

Over the years he had learned not to get his hopes up. By the fifth year he tried to act as if he were not hurt by the oversight. By year 10 he had mastered the art of pretending to be happy for all those who were invited. By year 15 he had become convinced he would never receive an invitation and had almost completely resigned himself to his current situation.

But this year was different, not because he knew or saw anything differently as it relates to his job performance or those senior to him in the company, but because his life had changed. His father had passed away, leaving him to care for and support his mother who was in failing health. Coupled with the ever-growing needs of his children and the ever-increasing expenses of life in general, he had come to realize that either he needed to move up soon or he would risk losing everything within two years.

The one thing he knew was that something had to change before things completely fell apart. His only hope was that this year would be different, that somehow he would go to the box and find his invitation there.

With a mix of hope and despair that only someone in his position could understand, he got up from his desk and walked towards the mailbox cubbies against the far wall. He could see that people had begun to gather together and that the invitations had in fact been delivered. He watched as one by one people walked up to their individual boxes and looked inside. Who had received an invitation and who hadn't was clear by their body language followed up by the traditional humility parade of the chosen few.

He finally made his way to his box and reached in but found only normal memos and paperwork--once again, no invitation. Once again passed over. He could feel the blood racing to his brain; it actually hurt to think. He walked back to his desk, picked up his backpack and walked out the door. He needed something to help him digest what had just happened.

Stepping into the elevator, grateful that he was the only one in the little square space, he pushed the lobby button. As the gears started to crank the box downwards, he changed his mind: he had had enough. He would go upstairs and give those folks a piece of his mind.

Chapter 24

Anne Madison had it made as a successful author, speaker and wife of a sitting senator. With all that in mind, her greatest joy was found in her two children, James and Bel. James was five years old and Annabel was the first to tell everyone that she was three and a half. Anne loved to spend time with them and went to bed looking forward to waking up to their boundless energy every morning. She often told her friends that she had gladly stopped all of her speaking and writing to spend time with her little ones. She was honestly amazed by the number of friends who didn't believe her and thought she only said those things because it was politically helpful to be the "loving mother."

This morning she rose to the sound of giggling as the children played "quietly" in their rooms until she woke up. They were amazing little humans who spent hours keeping busy by doing the most simple things. Stacking boxes wrapped in giftwrap would keep them happy for hours. They stacked them in different formations only to knock them down just so they could restack them again. One large sheet of paper and crayons would allow them to become artists working on a masterpiece creation.

The amount of joy and enthusiasm the two of them had made them more preferable to spend time with than almost any adult she knew.

She listened to their laughter flowing like bubbling streams and really hated to interrupt them with news that breakfast would be ready in a few minutes and they needed to wash their hands and get ready to eat. Their disappointment with having to stop playing was short-lived when they heard breakfast today was blueberry pancakes and if they hurried and washed up quickly they could help to make them into fun shapes. This bribery always seemed to work but Anne knew it worked because they really did want to help and be good. They loved their mother as much as she loved them. The only one that possibly and only possibly loved them more was their father.

After pancakes she loaded the children into the mini-van complete with what may be considered the greatest improvement in modern transportation: the car video system. Once it is engaged children are willing to ride in the car indefinitely or at least until their video ends. Driving with children in the car when Anne was a child meant arguments, pushing and lots of are-we-there-yet questions. Modern technology had made a car ride enjoyable as children recited the dialog from their favorite movies and sang along with every verse and chorus of the sound track.

This was particularly important when one lived in a city like Washington, where even the shortest of journeys can take forever. With the kids engrossed in their cartoon the 45-minute trip to the park would go quickly, at least for them. Traffic was actually moving at a much faster pace than usual. The usual bumper-to-bumper snail's pace movement was replaced by a breakneck speed of almost 35 miles per hour.

Anne turned her head just enough to speak to the children and let them know that the park was just over the hill. Her announcement was met with ear-to-ear grins and jumping for joy, at least all the jumping that James and Annabel could muster while tightly ensnared in their car seats. Like all parents,

Anne maintained a love-hate relationship with the car seat. Love because she like every other parent wanted the children safe; hate because every trip became a struggle as a result of the daily car seat battle royal, as neither child wanted to be strapped in. Every child's heart instinctively cries for freedom, and the car seat was man's best effort to stifle that cry.

Chapter 25

Thomas didn't need ten minutes to decide if he was going to accept the offer. As far as he was concerned he was in the driver's seat of this deal. It appeared he couldn't lose: he would not go to jail; his record would be expunged; he would receive a full pardon and all he had to do was undergo a battery of exams and tests to see if he qualified to work within the new but very hush-hush agency. The door opened and through it entered Senator Madison and two other men dressed with a similar sense of importance. He was introduced to the new arrivals: Madison's lawyer and a court- appointed attorney provided for him. Madison and his attorney remained standing.

With one glance Thomas knew that his lawyer was not a regular public defender. There was something about him that projected an air of exceptionalism. It wasn't just his clothing, but his presence spoke of experience and authority, two traits he had not seen in any public defenders in the past. After the introductions the senator and his lawyer walked out of the room leaving only Thomas and his "new" lawyer at the table.

The new lawyer wasted no time as he opened a file and pulled out a couple of documents to go over with Thomas. Thomas did his best to follow along as each paper was read and explained. It wasn't that he wasn't smart enough to understand, it was just that so much had happened in such a short period of time he was having difficulty processing all of the experience and information as quickly as it was being presented.

What he did know was that this appointed attorney was a high-dollar lawyer from one of the most prestigious firms in the D.C. area, who as a favor to the senator, had agreed to help out with this particular situation. William Cohan had an amazing way about him while it was clear that he was accomplished in his field from his manner and appearance. He spoke in a way that didn't make Thomas feel spoken down to. He had a gift that allowed him to treat people with respect to such a degree that even though it was clear he was doing a huge favor for both Thomas and Senator Madison, his disposition never made Thomas feel beholden in the process.

While he was explaining all of the ins and outs of the documents on the table, Thomas was really just interested in signing them and being released. Released normally would set him free, but just as he entertained that thought, he understood that signing these documents would not bring freedom but would only change by whom he was controlled. This thought didn't cause him to reconsider signing, but it did cause him to begin thinking about how he would have to establish a strategy to escape this bondage if necessary. After all, he didn't even know yet what he would be asked to do. Whatever it was, though, he knew it was a big enough deal for them to arrange his release.

The other thing he wondered about was how much this attorney actually knew about his situation and about his new employer. It seemed that there were times he acted and spoke like he knew everything and other times when it seemed as if he were fishing for information. Thomas decided that he would not share anything about the new agency and his involvement, which would be relatively easy because he really didn't have much information to share.

When all papers had been signed and countersigned, William Cohan arose to explain to Thomas that once they were processed he would be released and someone would meet him outside the jail to take him to his new home.

There were two developments Thomas didn't know about that resulted from his simple decision to keep total confidence. First was that he received a passing grade on the very first assessment of his training program. Second was that had he not passed, the paperwork would have been destroyed and everyone would have disavowed any knowledge of today's interaction. He would have been placed back in the holding cell and all of his charges would have been fully restored.

Chapter 26

As he emerged from the elevator for the very first time on the 30th floor, he looked ahead and saw the dutiful receptionist whose job it was to filter those who would be allowed into the inner sanctum of the executive suites from those who would be stopped as if they were attempting to cross an international border. She looked up for a moment towards Scott then lowered her head to glance at her computer screen once again. She didn't recognize the visitor, which meant he did not deserve any extraneous welcome from her. He would have to wait until he crossed the 40 feet between the elevator doors and the receptionist's desk.

As he walked across the expensive tile floor he wondered two things. First, how much money those floors cost to put down as compared to the ugly cheap commercial-grade carpet on the floors where the people labored who actually did the work. This expensive flooring was for those who did little more than direct the drones to the next task they would accomplish to bring even more money into the coffers of the nobles. The caste system had never been clearer to Scott than it was this very second.

His other thought was irrelevant to his situation or location, but he speculated upon it anyway and actually followed it up with a moment of further contemplation. Why when almost no one uses stairs anymore do people still say, "I am going upstairs or downstairs?" He had no idea why he was even entertaining something as trivial as that, but as he made his way up to the receptionist's desk his mind still ran with that thought.

So much so that when he came to a stop in front of the desk he had to refocus on his reason for coming upstairs to begin with. Gloria, the perfectly dressed young lady with immaculate makeup and hair, raised her head once again and in a tone that was both business-like and condescending asked, "How can I help you today?" Scott replied that he would like to speak to the vice president of operations, Mr. Carrington. Gloria continued in her role as guardian of the gate, "Do you have an appointment?" Scott responded, "No, but it is very important that I speak to him."

"Please have a seat while I see if Mr. Carrington will see you". Although it was a normal reply given in offices all over the city, this response seemed to be the last straw on Scott's back. "What do you mean-- 'if he will see me'?" Suddenly all his years of quiet servitude rushed like an ocean wave through his mind and out his mouth. His voice rose and his hands waved with more gusto than an air traffic controller as he vented all of his pent-up anger and pain.

While Gloria was used to a certain level of dissatisfied employees and clients, she had never seen this kind of an unleashed torrent of words and emotions before. She was unsure whether to call security or an ambulance or both. Slowly and without letting it be seen, she pushed the panic button just above her right knee on her desk that would alert security and management at the same time. This would also force the decision of who to call next to someone higher up the ladder of responsibility than herself.

In moments both the doors to the executive suites and the elevator opened. From one side two very large men in uniforms emerged and from the other Mr. Franks, a small man with wire-rimmed glasses and a crisp suit, came forth. While Mr. Franks, the office manager, who calmly approached Scott speaking in a soft but steady voice, drew Scott's attention, the two security guards swept up from behind and with swift but careful movements brought Scott's arms and to some extent his mind back into control.

Mr. Franks explained to Scott that due to his emotional state it would not be possible for him to speak with Mr. Carrington at this time, but that after calming down he should make an appointment and Mr. Carrington's assistant would be available to discuss whatever was on his mind. He further explained that the security team would help him to his car and that he should take the rest of the day off to recollect himself before returning to work after the weekend.

As he spoke those words, Mr. Franks knew that within just a few minutes the termination process of Scott Conner would be completed and that there would be no reason for him to either come to work

nor to make an appointment with Carrington's
assistant.

Chapter 27

As Thomas walked into the bright sunshine the first thing he saw was Senator Madison's limousine driving away into traffic. As he watched the car roll out of sight, a man walked up next to him and spoke quietly but forcefully in a way that reminded Thomas of how drill sergeants talked to recruits. He didn't introduce himself; he merely said, "Follow me," turned around and walked toward the courthouse parking lot.

Thomas stood still for just a moment before starting to walk in the same direction. There in front of him was a standard government issued cream-colored Ford Crown Victoria. The man opened the door, sat down and started the engine. Thomas had just reached the door and grabbed for the handle when the man said "Hurry up! We don't have all day."

Thomas quickly opened the door, slid smoothly into the seat and closed the door. He leaned back and waited to move, but the man just sat there staring at Thomas until he realized he was waiting for him to buckle his seat belt. Thomas reached for the belt behind his shoulder just as his new friend grunted, "Buckle up".

Thomas thought to himself, "I wonder where this guy left his personality" as they drove down the road without a word being spoken between them. Thomas had never felt so much like talking and so hesitant to do so at the same time.

The man driving was dressed in a suit, though not of the same caliber as the senator's or either of the lawyers Thomas had spent the afternoon with. As Thomas assessed the man he noted his suit was well pressed and fit him well but was clearly not tailored specially for him but had most likely been purchased right off the rack. His shoes were well cared for and polished but had clearly been worn for some time. His wristwatch was not cheap but also was not expensive. Thomas looked closer and saw that the man had scars on his hands and one on his face. This lead him to conclude he had been in his share of altercations, but the damage was minimal so he also concluded that he must have come out on top in most if not all of those fights. His hair was cut in a military style and he was clean-shaven, leading

Thomas to believe he was either active or prior military.

Not a word was spoken between the two until they pulled off the road and onto a winding driveway that led to a large building that looked like a cross between a school and an apartment house. The outside looked modest but well maintained. It had a large landscaped lawn with neatly trimmed shrubs surrounding the circular driveway. As they pulled to a stop behind two other vehicles his driver opened the door and with the same half-grunt said, "Get out."

It wasn't until just then that Thomas realized that not only did he not know where he was, but he also didn't have anything with him. He was, as they say, left with only the shirt on his back. He opened his door and stood up. Just to let the driver know that he was not going to be pushed around, he walked onto the grass and stretched, twisting and turning and bending his knees, not for a long time, but just long enough to establish that he was doing something he wanted to do.

After waiting a few moments for Thomas to finish,

with a slight grin on his face the man said, "Let's go, one more time," and up the stairs they went towards a large wooden doorway. Just as they stepped in front of the door it opened and a man dressed in similar fashion to the driver walked forward, stuck out his hand and introduced himself as Dillon Chambers. "I will be your senior assessor during your training," he said. "You have already met Joshua Jacobs. I'm sure you have a lot of questions and knowing Joshua, you had very little conversation during the trip in."

Chapter 28

Senator Madison was seated at his desk studying one of the hundreds of proposals that crossed his workspace each day. The average American citizen had no idea how many pages of information a senator had to review, and these were only the papers that had already gone through the crucible of his staff. If it weren't for his staff reading through and providing outlines and notes on each document, like every other congressman he would do nothing each day except read and re-read proposal after proposal, each one containing hundred of pages of legalese, which even the lawyers could hardly understand.

He was glad when he heard the knock on his door. Looking up he saw his chief of staff entering the room carrying another folder in his hand, except this folder was red, so Madison knew it had to do with the Thomas project.

Bob Johnson had been serving as Madison's chief of staff since he entered politics. He was the only person besides his wife that Madison truly trusted.

Bob walked to the desk and opened the folder and began to explain that Homeland Security had received a credible report about an Islamic entering the country via the Mexican border and had since made his way to New York City. The intelligence provided his name and his intended target--a Metro station in Washington.

After a quick look at the intelligence report, Madison instructed Johnson to assemble the staff in the conference room. A few minutes' later two men and one woman entered the conference room and sat down across the desk.

At first glance none of these staffers would have been taken for some of the most important people in Washington. Each one looked as if he would have been much more comfortable sitting in front of a computer terminal typing out code than sitting in a senators office. Truthfully, they were all top caliber analysts who did spend their time staring at computer screens. Their job as members of the staff was to find simple solutions to complex problems. The elaborate problems they regularly dealt with would make the difference between life and death sometimes for individuals and sometimes, as in this case, for thousands of people.

After the team was briefed on the situation, Madison and Johnson left the room and let them do what they did best: think outside the lines and find a way to interact with the situation and change one item in such a way as to effect the outcome.

How best to stop a terrorist without injury to the terrorist if possible and to any of the prospective targets, while at the same time limiting exposure of the agency – this was their current challenge. They had met like this before and each time they had been able to locate one key change that while not being noticed, would provide a significant change to the end result: lives saved and bad guys caught or eliminated.

This team knew how something as simple as a flat tire at just the right moment, or a soda can being stuck in a vending machine, for example, could effect time and time could effect change to almost every situation. It was, after all, the little things that brought about real change.

In this case, they were scouring videotapes taken by surveillance cameras located all around the city, watching for the presence of the now-known terrorist. Their job this time was a little easier than some of their previous operations, for this time they knew their subject would be purchasing a train ticket. That narrowed down the search areas considerably. Jane Bryan, a forty-year old woman with a doctorate degree in theology and the sole woman on the team, was first to spot their target at a ticket counter.

Her participation on the team was always a source of humor to the two men who served with her. Paul West, a former music professor, and Yitzak Goldman, a chemical engineer raised in an orthodox Jewish community but who had walked away from Judaism when it seemed science provided more answers than Scripture. Jane was full of faith and confidence in God's design of all things while Yitzak believed that everything in the universe existed because of evolution and happenstance. Paul viewed the world as a beautiful symphony whose composer was either unknown or unknowable.

The differing academic backgrounds of the team members always made Senator Madison smile. When he began to assemble the team he had searched for applicants whose academic backgrounds focused on research, but he found that most of them were great at searching for something only when they knew what was being searched for. Unfortunately they had done poorly at figuring out the initial target of a search. In other words, they could find the perfect hamburger if they were told to find it, but they could never decide they needed a hamburger.

It was at the urging of Bob Simon that Madison decided to look outside of the box when he found Bryan, Goldman and West. The three of them from vastly different disciplines had amazing abilities to look at data and find things no one else was able to see.

After making sure it was indeed their subject on the video, they began to count how many other people had purchased tickets from the opening of the day. This information was necessary and needed to be completely accurate if their operation was to be successful. The three of them took turns viewing the tape and counting each ticket sold. The number was much smaller than it could have been; thankfully, the transaction occurred early in the shift. The 347th ticket delivered.

Chapter 29

The lab was unusually quiet as Dr. Reading prepared for the first human test of his invention. It had worked perfectly on all prior living test subjects, but now the real test would take place. The machine was smaller than he originally anticipated as technology had continued to allow greater things to be accomplished with ever-shrinking components.

In the lab room itself were only three people: Matthew, his lab assistant and Thomas. Watching from an observation room above the lab sat Senator Madison, his chief of staff and Dillon Chambers, who had transported Thomas to the facility.

Emotions for each man were riding high for differing reasons. Matthew was wound as tightly as he had ever been. Everything he had worked for on the project was about to be tested. He knew inside that there was no room for error because a human life was in his hands. It would either work perfectly or Matthew would consider it a failure. Thomas' thoughts were running in a different direction although he also knew that the trial run held his life in its hands. His mind raced back to that room in the courthouse on the day he had first met Senator Madison. He couldn't help but think of the reference to the movie "The Matrix," and wonder if he had taken the wrong pill. The Senator was more pragmatic about the test. He had already discussed a less than perfect outcome with Chambers and the possible need for a replacement for Thomas. He knew the device worked, but just may not have been perfected yet. His last thought before Matthew pressed the enter button on his keyboard was, "If at first you don't succeed--try, try again."

Everyone watching except Dr. Reading was surprised by the silence as the test began. After so many years of sci-fi movies they expected a loud buzzing sound to coincide with a great flash of light, or something equally dramatic. Instead those witnessing the event heard and saw nothing at all, including Thomas, who was no longer in the lab with them. If any of them had sneezed they would have missed the entire experience. For a moment no one moved at all and in all honesty no one really knew if the test was successful or not. They just kept staring at the place where Thomas had been and now was not. No one spoke, moved or even blinked any more than necessary as they waited for the completion of the test, because Thomas' disappearance was not the entire goal of the test. A successful result would only be achieved when Thomas was returned and was without damage from the process.

Chapter 30

Abdul Nader was an average young Iraqi man until an American missile launch from a drone took the life of his older brother Hakeem. From that moment on, his hatred for the United States grew like a snowball rolling down a hill. It didn't matter to Abdul that Hakeem was an active part of the insurgency, nor did it make any difference that Abdul was not a devout Muslim himself. He just hated the people who took his brother from him.

This hatred made Abdul a prime target for indoctrination by what are known in the West as radical organizations, although the members of these groups would not consider themselves radical in the least.

It didn't take those in leadership to recognize that Abdul was exactly the type of young man they were looking for. His hatred and aggressive personality made him pliable and his intelligence level made him trainable.

Once they established his place within the ranks of their faction, he began intensive training in weapons and explosives as well as physical training to achieve the necessary level of fitness required to fulfill his mission.

Although he had learned English in school, he spent long hours practicing to speak without a discernable accent. This took great effort as each word and sound had to be adjusted so that not only did he not sound Iraqi, but he also didn't want to stand out with a regional American accent.

Beyond working on speaking English like an American he also was required to speak Spanish with a Mexican accent. This way his access into the United States would not be hampered either within Central America or at the Texas border or in his involvement with the coyotes (human transporters) that would provide passage for him into Texas. The fewer people questioning where he came from, the fewer problems Abdul would have in what would be the most difficult part of his mission.

His training went better than anyone had expected and within just over nine months he was ready to travel into America. He would take a car out of Iraq into Saudi Arabia, then board a freighter from Saudi to Panama. From Panama he would make his way through Costa Rica, Nicaragua, Honduras, Guatemala and finally across Mexico.

Abdul had memorized the names and locations of contacts at each point on his journey. It had been pressed into his mind that he would be allowed to have nothing written down that could be found by authorities in any of the countries he would be traveling on the slim chance that someone along the way would be taking the war on terror seriously.

Chapter 31

There are few things more personally dissatisfying than suddenly being woke up by the loud siren sounds accompanied by flashing lights. Yet this was only one example of the training techniques Thomas had to endure. While he didn't fully understand each of the different aspects of his training, he did understand that if he were to be accepted into the program he would have to tolerate the discomforts he was being exposed to.

Thomas' training regimen was much more elaborate than he ever expected. He had never served in the military but was convinced those who had didn't have to go through a boot camp like this one.

His normal day, if one could call it that, began with a five-mile run followed by a cliff climb. After he completed the climb, he would then repel down the cliff and start running back to his training barracks where he would do calisthenics. At 6:30 he would eat breakfast and then begin his swimming portion of the training, which involved being dropped into the ocean water from a helicopter with instructions to swim home.

After arriving back at the training facility he would eat lunch and start a regimen of activities ranging from standing perfectly still to hanging upside down for extended periods of time. He also had learned to move as stealthily as a cat: moving without producing a sound; walking like a ghost into and out of rooms.

But the most difficult part of the training for Thomas was learning how to do what his instructors termed "walking in the light." This involved paying constant attention to all sources of light so that anytime he traveled from one location to another he minimized the amount of shadow he projected. A zero shadow level was the desired goal. No matter how busy someone was a shadow movement drew peripheral attention. A shadow was always seen more noticeably than what actually caused it.

After his morning fitness routine Thomas spent the rest of the day practicing his shadow techniques. He walked into and out of the same series of rooms under the watchful eyes of his team of Chambers and Jacobs, with each man looking for any hint of a shadow. But it was not enough to trust fully in the human ability to discern the presence of a shadow. Chambers' technical team had formatted cameras and a computer program that would identify shadows that could possibly be missed by even the most careful human optical scan.

Although to the casual observer the exercise seemed horribly redundant, Chambers knew that each and every time with the change of the sun's location and the movements of cloud cover, the light was slightly different and made each entry from room to room unique.

Chambers also knew that if Thomas were going to succeed in his missions he not only had to be able to blend into his environment --he was already notoriously good at that-- he also had to not alter his environment, which was what they were working very hard to teach him now.

Every part of the training served a purpose and was designed by specialists to maximize the trainee's ability to impact a situation while limiting his impact on his surroundings. Each physical task was calculated to conform Thomas into a precision tool that could undertake a specific mission no matter what level of physical, emotional or psychological impediments came into play.

Thomas did not know the purpose of the sudden wake-ups, the cliff climbing, the repelling, and swimming and the many other "training opportunities" he was being required to withstand. But each of the tasks and his physical, physiological and psychological responses to each were being carefully monitored.

Chapter 32

Bob Johnson came rushing through the office door. For the first time in his position as chief of staff for Senator Madison he had not knocked on the door. The look on his face was an expression of panic that Madison had never seen before on his right-hand man. His mind raced to the terrorist threat and he immediately wondered if they had been too late to interject into the plot the solution that had been decided upon by his team.

Johnson walked directly up to the desk and told his boss to please sit down. He then did his best to share the news that he had just received from the Metropolitan Police Department. His wife Anne and their two children had just been in a terrible accident. They were being transported by helicopter to George Washington Hospital. The report was that all three were in critical condition.

Madison did his best to stand to his feet and head to the hospital, but for some reason he could not feel his legs. As he lifted his body nothing below his waist responded and then everything went dark. He came to moments later and when he saw Bob's face he knew it was not a dream. He was then able with help to stand up and gather his thoughts. He grabbed his coat and with Bob at his side strode towards his car. As he walked through the office he could see the tears in the eyes of those standing and watching. He knew they knew and for the first time in a long time he hoped that someone was praying.

It was that thought that seemed to pierce his mind at that moment. The most important things in his life were in danger and the only thing he could think to do was to get to them and prayer. He had not prayed in years. He had been involved in situations that imperiled the globe and he didn't pray. He was intimately involved in the decisions about conflicts and wars the world over and prayer was never on his mind.

As with all politicians he spoke of prayer at times of distress, natural disasters, at the passing of people of importance, but those were platitudes that brought comfort to his constituents and brought a connection to his conservative base.

But to actually respond to a situation with a heartfelt desire to somehow connect to God had been outside of his nature and honestly, he thought it was outside of his beliefs. Until just now, when he all at once understood the old adage that there were no atheists in foxholes. He realized without warning that for the first time in his life he was in a foxhole.

They arrived quickly at the hospital and were rushed directly to a special section of the emergency room reserved for people who needed both the excellent care provided at GWU as well as extra security required by people in the highest levels of government and their families.

He had been in hospitals many times during his life, visiting family members and friends and even at the births of his children. In all of those visits he never really noticed all of the lights and sounds all around him. Monitors flashed, LCD displays of numbers, even the fluorescent bulbs on the ceiling seemed to be brighter and buzz louder.

As he turned the corner around the nurses' station he came face to face with the head of emergency medicine. By the look on his face he knew without a word being uttered that things were not good. The doctor provided a report of the information available at the moment. His wife and children were all in different operating rooms, each being treated for severe trauma. They each had multiple broken bones and the level of internal and organ damage had not yet been fully determined. They had each lost a lot of blood and although there was hope, he didn't want to sugarcoat the reality of the situation.

Chapter 33

When Thomas arrived at the Legacy Hotel at 5:00 p.m., he immediately knew two things: first, that this was clearly a hotel that he would have never chosen to stay at; and second, that he was glad that in this case he should not have to spend much time here. He wondered for a split second what the legacy of this dump of a hotel was?

Thomas had only moments to walk out of the office and make his way to the street before the manager was to return from his dinner break. He made his way to the door and was glad that people usually only put locks on doors to keep people out of places so he simply had to turn the lock and walk out of the small filthy office.

It was only twenty feet to go out the front door and onto the street. Rarely would Thomas have enjoyed the surroundings of this particular street with its dumpsters, trash and broken down buildings, but coming out of the Legacy even this street was a step up.

He only had a few blocks to walk to get to the subway station where the second third of today's assignment would take place. He walked down the road quickly enough to get where he needed in a timely manner but slowly enough so that no one on the street would take notice of his having been there. This gait was not something he learned in training for his current position but something he had taught himself in his previous career path.

He arrived at the Benning Road Metro station right on time for shift change and made his way to the ticket booth. During shift change was the best time to do what needed to be done because those arriving were just getting started and those leaving just wanted to go. No one would be standing around with nothing to do but to watch what would be going on. Dressed in a uniform of the Washington Metropolitan Area Transit Authority with an official photo ID badge, Thomas was immediately let into the booth.

One of the best things about working for a covert government agency was that you never had any problems acquiring official photo ID cards and you didn't have to pay top dollar for counterfeit. You actually just obtained a real one ordered from the actual agency.

He walked into the booth and explained he was there to change out the ticket machine. In a very casual way, he told them that someone in an office somewhere had decided that instead of waiting for the machines to break and slow down customer service; they would rotate the machines in and out for preventative maintenance.

It was always worth a laugh among civil servants whenever you could comment about someone in an office having a thought, especially when it was a thought that made sense and actually could be helpful to those working in the trenches.

Thomas walked directly up to his assigned ticket machine and proceeded to unplug it, disconnect it from the computer terminal, and replace it with one that looked identical. Again, working for the government allowed him to requisition the exact units used by the transit authority. This machine was exactly the same in every respect, down to and including the number of tickets loaded; exactly the same except for one ticket--the 347th ticket in the machine.

After replacing the unit, Thomas made another passing joke about those people sitting downtown who behaved as if they knew what it was like to knuckle down to a real day's work, all the while knowing that while the people in the booth all expected that someone doing what he was doing would be speaking to them, not one of them would really care to listen and no one would actually hear what he was saying. They would only know that he had been there; he had said something; and he changed out the machine for servicing. Oh, and that someone in an office downtown may have actually done something helpful for a change.

Chapter 34

Scott Conner sat almost frozen in the driver's seat of his decade-old Honda Civic, his mind inundated with so many thoughts that he was not able to processing them into anything rational. He could not remember ever being as angry as he was at this very moment. He was not sure if he was madder because of the level of embarrassment he had just endured or if it was just the years of pent-up rage that burst forth in the executive suites.

Make an appointment next week, really! Make an appointment? Did they really think he was that stupid? He knew his career was over. In all reality he would be un-employable anywhere if his references were checked.

He reviewed all the events of the past few hours to see if anywhere within his memory was to be found a bit of hope. But he could not find any.

He turned the key in his ignition but instead of the sound of a four-cylinder motor roaring to life, he only heard the click...click of a dead battery. He reached under the dash to pull the hood release and with a slam of his door, exited the car to do the same thing he had been doing for months: jiggle the terminal-end connection on the battery. After a few attempts of jiggling the connections and turning the key, the car finally started and he pulled into the traffic for his ride home.

His thoughts now turned from the events of the day at the office to what he would face at home when he arrived. Now his emotions of anger mixed with embarrassment had been joined with the addition of fear. How was he going to be able to explain to his wife that he had lost his job? How was he going to pay the bills now? How could he have been so out of control that he didn't consider the implications of his actions?

All of these thoughts merged with his previous swirl of deliberations and in the midst of his mind nearly exploding, Scott didn't even see the light turn red and it wasn't until it was too late that he saw the mini-van crossing in front of him. His feet and hands moved as fast as humanly possible to stomp on the brake pedal while he turned the steering wheel as hard as he could.

Scott was not sure how or why but he was certain that he heard the sounds of crashing glass and bending metal before he felt the cars come into contact with each other. He also saw a scene that he knew if he survived he would never be able to erase from his mind: the faces of a mother and her two children as they watched his car careen into their van. They were not the faces of fear or anger but more looks of disbelief, especially, on the children. He could almost see them asking, "Why is this man driving his car into us"?

Chapter 35

Abdul woke up just as he did every day since arriving in America: to the sound of the television. Like many people who come to America, he was surprised by the amount of channels at one's disposal. The hotel he was staying in had a cable system with almost 1000 channels available. He wondered to himself why--no one could watch more than one program at a time, and from his limited knowledge most of the shows seemed very much the same with different actors and settings but the same plots.

Nevertheless, he still watched and for a reason he could not put a handle on, derived a weird sense of comfort while sleeping with the sounds of the television on as background noise.

He looked at the calendar and confirmed the date. His mission had been painstakingly planned down to the minute so that his actions would bring the greatest impact. He arrived at the appointed time; stayed at the chosen hotel; wore the clothing that had been provided; ate at the restaurants previously picked out. Truly, he could not think of one thing he had done since arriving in the United States that wasn't preprogrammed for him by his handlers with the exception of watching television. Maybe that was the reason for his subconscious level of comfort. The TV was the only thing he was doing that was under his own control.

Other than going to the assigned restaurants, the only tasking he was responsible for today was to purchase a Metro ticket. He got up and took a hot shower, an experience he had grown to appreciate since in Iraq a hot bath involved carrying water from a well and heating it up on a fire. The simplicity of turning on a faucet and being able to adjust the water to a preferred temperature was a luxury of which he had become very fond.

After getting dressed he made his way to the Benning Road Metro station and stood in line. He looked just like every other person in line, not so much in how he dressed because the people in line were all dressed differently. There were businessmen in classic suits and young people wearing what he had learned was referred to as urban wear. The sameness came not in their dress but rather in their mannerisms. They all stood with the same level of impatience: everything from how they stood, the looks on their faces, the way they tapped their fingers on their arms. They all wanted to be somewhere else and were only here because in order to get there they had to be here. No one wanted to be standing in that line. They were all in a hurry and their body language made it clear to everyone.

It was a universal truth that when you were the only place to get something that everyone needed, that you need not be concerned with customer service. While every ticket agent knew that the people standing in line could not purchase the tickets anywhere else, they also knew they had eight hours on their shift so they were in absolutely no hurry to process the sales.

Abdul finally made his way to the front of the line and purchased his ticket. He had heard it said that purchasing a travel ticket is the first step to changing your life. Abdul knew this one would change his life but he didn't know how dramatically it would.

Chapter 36

It was almost two hours from when he first arrived that Senator Madison looked up to see the doctor walking towards him again. One of the unique things about hospital waiting rooms is that most of the people in them are caught in a strange place: starving for information about their loved one's condition while at the same time not sure they really want to hear the report.

As the doctor approached, Madison scanned his face for a sign of the content of the report he was about to receive. The doctor pulled up a chair close to him and started to go over all of the details of the status of his family. He started out by saying that all three were still critical and that it would be many hours and possibly several more surgeries each before they would be out of the woods.

James knew that each word the doctor was speaking to him was about people he loved more than anything on earth, yet he could not focus on what was being said. The feeling of being totally at a loss in a situation was relatively new to him. His life up to this point had been a series of controlled events, starting with his nursery school and leading up to his graduation from university. He had never experienced disruption to the degree that he was right now.

His life had been charted by his parents from cradle until entry into public service. Upon entering the world of politics he had handlers to make sure everything was managed to achieve the desired outcome. Even his wife was one of the women deemed acceptable and profitable toward his image. Like most men of his position, many of his choices were never really his choice.

The choice of Anne, though not completely his, was in fact a choice he did want to make. He had fallen head over heels in love with her from the moment he first laid eyes on her. She was the first woman he had ever met that made his heart skip a beat when he got close to her and after almost a decade of marriage he still felt the same way about her. Now she was lying in an ICU ward bed, in effect drifting between life and death--and he could do nothing about it. His attention was once again drawn back to the sound of the doctor's voice as if suddenly someone tuned in to a radio station. The doctor was conveying his report in very thorough details, updating him on the condition of both his wife and his children.

He kept thinking about how powerless he was to help his family, that despite all of his resources and the best medical care money could buy he could lose everyone he loved because of one person's carelessness.

It wasn't until that very moment that he realized he was not powerless, nor did he have to accept the conclusion of the doctors or anyone else telling him how hopeless this situation was. He was possibly the only person in a position to save his family.

He looked directly into the doctors eyes and spoke softly, "Please do everything you can to treat them no matter what the cost." He stood up and spoke to Bob, "Please assemble the staff."

Chapter 37

Officer Ron Blackman looked at the screen of the computer in his patrol car and the latest entry, which was flashing red. He thought back briefly to the time before computers when there were no real time updates about the different calls and whom they were assigned to. Not only did they instantly know what a call was and who was involved, they could also at the push of a button to see if the people involved had previous contacts with law enforcement and if they did what that contact involved.

Although being a cop was still dangerous, technology had reduced some of the unknown factors and made it possible for officers to not enter situations completely blind.

One of the points of information presented on screen was provided by the colors assigned to each call. Green calls meant that there was a report but whatever was reported was no longer happening and in most cases, it was what was known as a report call. This included things like car burglary or vandalism; the people who committed the crimes had long since left the scene. Green calls were considered low priority, not necessarily unimportant but they just were responded to after higher priority calls. Yellow was the color designation for active but not life-threatening calls: security alarms going off or shoplifting in progress. These were timely calls with the possibility of catching the criminal in the act sufficient enough to drive expeditiously to the location, but not serious enough for lights and sirens.

When red showed up on the screen it meant that something life-threatening was happening: a kidnapping in progress or an armed robbery or an officer in distress would bring the flashing red lights on the screen. These calls brought immediate response. Officers knew that once they saw red they were to proceed with all due haste to the location, lights flashing, siren screaming and driving as fast as possible while also being as safe as possible. Lives were on the line and moments could make the difference between a positive outcome and a tragedy. So when Ron looked down at the screen and saw the red appear he immediately turned his cruiser around and headed towards the Metro station.

He clicked on the red line on his screen and noticed that the reporting agency was Homeland Security. It provided only a photograph of Abdul Nader, an Iraqi national, a "high value" person of interest wanted for questioning. He was classified as possibly armed and dangerous. The BOLO (Be on the Look out) instructions said to proceed with caution and report contact to Homeland Security. Ron understood that high value was Homeland Security code for a terrorist or at least someone with strong ties to terrorism. The information screen provided what appeared to be a passport photo and his last-known location, which appeared to be in the direction of the Benning Road Metro station.

Ron pulled his cruiser right into the no-parking area in front of the Metro entrance. After radioing his arrival to dispatch, he made his way through the doors and down the stairs towards the Metro. As he walked he scanned back and forth looking for the subject. With hundreds of people walking in all directions he knew it would be like finding a needle in a haystack. He was determined to find Nader even if he had no idea what he had done or was planning to do. What he did know was that Homeland Security placed him as a high-priority find. He looked around. Within moments of his arrival more than a dozen other officers were on scene and scanning the area with the same intensity he was. He was sure that beyond the number of police in the station there would be additional officers stationed at all entrances and exits, creating a containment perimeter.

Chapter 38

Thomas arrived to find himself in a small room with simple furniture. There was a wooden desk, a cloth chair, and a small well-worn sofa that may have been able to seat two people if they were very friendly. Across the room from the couch was a small television stand and an old television. Whoever's office this was hadn't even modernized to a flat screen. He looked at the television to see what program was on. It surprised him a little that it was turned to the Discovery Channel and an episode about Dr. Reading and his work with NASA. He thought to himself--if a well-decorated office was the sign of a successful man then how unsuccessful did someone have to be to rate this office? After watching the program for a few seconds he recognized that the office he had entered into was the office on the program!

He felt fine except for a buzzing sensation in his head and throughout his whole body. The closest thing he could relate it to was the feeling he had after using his father's electric hedge trimmers one afternoon, a steady vibration that seemed to stay with him for hours after he finished trimming all of the hedges.

It took him a moment to acclimate to his new surroundings. He then removed a copy of the day's newspaper and took a pen out of his pocket to draw a mustache on the face of the president, whose picture was on the front page.

After completing an artful job on the mustache, he replaced the pen in his pocket, placed the newspaper back on the desk, walked across the room towards the television then glanced at his wristwatch and pressed the button hidden on the side.

He looked back up again and upon feeling the same buzzing sensation he realized he was back in Dr. Reading's lab. It happened so fast that he had to wonder if it really happened at all.

Dr. Reading walked over to Thomas and began to examine him, asking all kinds of questions. What day was it? Who was president? How old are you?

What is your name? After asking a battery of questions to make sure that Thomas' faculties were in order, his disposition changed from concerned doctor to excited like a child after his first roller coaster ride. He no longer was asking for scientific reasons but began to question him about the test. What was it like? What did he see? Did he feel anything special?

The truth was Thomas didn't really know how he felt. He knew the test was a success so he felt a sense of joy in that. He realized in his limited knowledge that everything seemed to function as it should. He felt exactly as a pilot must feel after finishing all of the ground training and finally being able to sit behind the stick and fly a plane. Or maybe it was more like a skydiver who after all of his ground training finally took that step out of an airplane and experienced the sudden jerking of the parachute opening then the extreme calm of floating completely free of all connections down to the earth.

He had completed his training, physical and mental. Now he had actually been able to do what he had been trained for. Now he had free-fallen for the first time and it was exhilarating and even more so than with experimental pilots or with the first man to ever strap on a parachute. He was the first person ever to be transported in this way.

Chapter 39

The team had assembled back at the office when Senator Madison came into the room with a file folder and placed it on the desk. As he did he looked directly into the eyes of each of the team members to let them know that he knew that they knew about his wife and children. Without even anyone saying a word he knew all of the things that they would have said and they knew he appreciated their thoughts and prayers.

The file contained all of the information available on the life of the new subject/project that they would be working on. When Madison put together this team he knew they were the best of the best researchers who, if it were possible, could identify a single moment in time when if one word was not spoken, or if a particular action did or didn't take place a situation could be corrected or an event could be stopped completely.

Imagine if you would a serial murderer like Ted Bundy, who before his execution revealed that his addiction to pornography was what drove him to rape and murder. He could have been stopped--not by the death penalty, but by removing his first exposure to pornography. That single change could have saved all of the lives of the young women he killed as well as Bundy's life also.

World War I could have been prevented not with greater military force but simply by stopping the death of one person: Archduke Franz Ferdinand of Austria. With the resources available through computers, the Internet and Dr. Reading's machine, Madison realized that his team could find these singularities; and by making small unnoticeable changes, change the course of human events.

It would be easy to find the person who committed whatever horrible act the team was trying to stop and just arrange an accident or have an assassin take the person out. But that went directly against Madison's pacifism. He had found a way to interject someone into almost any situation to change a singularity and by doing so, prevent something horrible from happening and keep someone from becoming horrible at the same time.

The team had worked on many situations with complete success; however, this particular subject was more than just an unknown name and photo in a file. This was Scott Conner, the man that had sent his car careening into Madison's family just hours ago.

While they always understood their rolls in each of the missions to which they had been assigned, they had never had a personal stake in any of them. These were research projects; information on computer screens and in file folders far removed from their personal lives and feelings. This time, though, was different. This time they were having a hard time finding a good reason for not just picking a time and place to send that assassin to take this subject out.

Knowing that his team would rightfully feel this way, Madison stopped to remind them that every situation like the one he was dealing with was caused by a human being, and that humans' actions were always the result or a response to circumstances, which, if changed, would not have transpired. You know when bad things happen to good people and then they cause bad things to happen to good people? Well, they were in a position to remove the bad thing, that which happened to Conner, which would stop the bad things from happening to his family. He instructed them to find the singularity that would right the wrong so they could save the lives of all involved.

Chapter 40

Abdul looked into his mirror with a great deal of happiness: the day had arrived when he would finally get revenge for the death of his brother. He knew everything was in order and that he had accomplished everything exactly as instructed. In just a couple hours he would pick up the backpack with the bomb in it. He would walk to the Metro station and sit on a bench waiting until the perfect time when, at the busiest time of the day, he would simply walk away, leave the bag behind him and go home.

Home--not to his apartment here in Washington--but back home to Iraq. He would miss some of the luxuries he had grown accustomed to in America: hot and cold running water; air-conditioning; and bars, to name three things off the top of his head. But it would be good to be home back with his family and away from the people he hated so much. He had only been in the USA for a short time but in that time he grew to hate America and Americans even more than he did after the death of his brother.

He could not understand a country where so many people had so much but were never satisfied. People used the freedoms they had to amass great wealth that people in Iraq never even dreamed of having and then spent all of their time complaining about the very laws and lifestyle that allowed them to achieve what they had. People would send their military to other lands to set people free and then attack the very freedoms they were exporting. He remembered when the USA "set Iraq free" and then desired to establish a democratic government and set in place a new constitution. Everyone in Iraq laughed that it didn't seem to anyone in the U.S. government that the constitution of the United States was good enough to pattern Iraq's new constitution after. Instead they tried to blend constitutions from many other countries into one that could fit the people of Iraq and their unique needs. The Iraqis all wondered why if the United States was such a land of freedom and prosperity, that they would not have patterned the Iraqi constitution after the one that established those freedoms. After all, it was adherence to that constitution that made the United States as powerful as it was.

It was this strange love/hate relationship the people of the United States had with their country that added to the hatred Abdul had for them. His brother had been killed in the name of freedom for Iraq, and the very country that proposed and fought to force those western values on Iraq was in constant battle to free itself from the very freedoms it was exporting to other countries.

Yes, he would be glad to be home, back to a place that, though far from perfect, at least made sense. Iraq was a violent place filled with religious fanatics, but at least when they fought they actually believed in what they were fighting for. In the USA, faith and freedom were things people sang songs about and at moments of crisis, people would turn to their houses of worship. But within hours of the end of the crisis they went back to living their lives in the same way they did before. The convictions and faith turned on and off like their hot and cold water. Although Abdul was not a religious man, he didn't hypocritically claim that he was unlike those in the United States, who proclaimed to be a Judeo/Christian society and yet espoused lifestyles that were condemned by the teachings of the Book that Jews and Christians there claimed to believe. This self-deception was the very thing that Abdul believed would eventually bring the destruction of America and the opening of doors to domination by Islamic nations. Even though Abdul didn't believe their teachings, at least those who said they believed followed the teachings they professed.

It was because of this double-mindedness of the United States' people and government that Abdul was able to so easily enter the country. While the USA proclaimed to follow the laws established by the government, the Immigration laws had long since stopped being enforced. This change of policy was not done through the court system or through legislation but simply by executive decision of the President, something that violated the very constitution that the President and Congress swore to uphold and defend. Though clearly illegal and unconstitutionally established, this policy was put in place simply because those in power and those who put them in power didn't really care about being constitutional anymore. The laws designed to protect America from illegal immigration were no longer being enforced, which left the door wide open for Abdul and others like him to rain terror on the country. Yes, Abdul thought, it would be good to be back home in a land where although things were difficult they made more sense, at least to him.

Chapter 41

Senator Madison and Bob Johnson stood in the observation room and looked at each other at the same instant for some sign that both of them had seen the same things happen. Neither one wanted to be the first to say something while both of them clearly were in a state of amazed shock. It appeared that the machine had completed its first actual live human test. After testing it first on inanimate objects, then dead animals, and then on living animals, and now finally on a living human subject, from all visible signs, it was a complete success. They watched from their perch as Thomas was standing in front of them just yards away and suddenly was gone and then moments later, returned to be standing before their eyes.

They both viewed the event with what Madison had termed confident fear. He had the utmost confidence in Dr. Reading and his research and development team. All the previous tests had been successful but this one was different. This time a living human subject had been transferred and returned.

They looked at each other for a few moments then smiled and rose up from their seats, not sure what the appropriate response to the successful test should be. They started to step forward for what at first looked like was going to be a high-five, which morphed into a simple handshake and finally, once they realized no one was looking, a congratulatory hug.

They walked out of the observation room down the steel staircase and into the laboratory door, where Dr. Reading and Thomas were both looking as if they had just scored the winning touchdown in the Super Bowl, only they knew what had just happened was much more important than any ballgame would ever be. This simple test known about by only a handful of people had the ability to save the lives of millions of people and change the very dynamics of society.

Dr. Reading stopped speaking to Thomas and turned to Madison. With a smile that would have made the Cheshire cat proud, he stepped forward and prepared to give his report. After his cursory examination of Thomas it appeared that there were no noticeable adverse effects caused from the machine.

He did, however, make sure that the senator understood that although it appeared that Thomas' first mission was a success, they would not know complete results until they travelled to Dr. Reading's office to see if Thomas had in fact completed his mission and if the machine had in fact been able to function as it was designed to.

They half-walked, half-ran out of the lab and down the long hall that separated the labs from the office suites, suites being a very generous term for what served as offices for those on Dr. Reading's team. Dr. Reading had not entered his office for a week and the video cameras strategically located in and around the building would have their recordings reviewed and documented as part of the test record.

Once the door was unlocked by a security guard they walked into the room and on the center of the desk was a copy of the daily newspaper, with a photo of the president sporting a mustache drawn with a sharpie marker. The presence of the newspaper would not have been relevant normally, but this paper was this morning's edition and no one had entered through the door since last week. This paper was also different because Thomas had added the mustache to the front page himself as an additional method of proving the machine worked. Neither, Madison nor Reading had known that Thomas would provide this additional proof of the success of the machine.

After seeing the newspaper they now were completely confident in the ability of the machine to make it possible for them to effect positive change in the world, in a way far more expansive than ever possible before. They could change things after they had happened; they now had the ability to transport people from one time to another.

Chapter 42

The team had spent nearly 24 hours investigating Scott Conner, his life, and his family; everything about him from the day he was born until today. The average American would be shocked by the amount of information available on the Internet. A simple search engine search can provide a wealth of personal information readily available to anyone with Internet access. On top of that, people assist those looking for private information by providing an open door to their lives through social media outlets like Facebook and Twitter. These not only provide birthdates, anniversaries and a history of relationships, they also provide an array of photos of the page holder and all of their friends. On top of all the open-access information freely available, those working within government programs and those with security clearances can reach over the walls which once provided a citizen his rights of privacy. At one time protected by all means necessary, these rights had been breached by the very government agencies tasked with protecting its citizens. With the advance of computer memories and programming, the government now could not only access and read emails, text messages and phone records, but had the ability to store this information in massive data warehouses, which could then be researched through information-capturing algorithms that in well-trained hands could piece together a person's life from cradle to grave.

It was with this type of access the team searched the entire life of American citizen Scott Conner. They did not have a warrant allowing them access to personal files, bank accounts, email, or phone records. One reason was that it would be impossible to get a judge to sign a warrant needed for such a broad search and another reason is that no one outside of Senator Madison and his team actually knew anything about this program and the mechanism in place for it to function.

The team searched file after file, looking for one point they could identify that would allow them to make a change small enough to effect the needed adjustment while not large enough to cause significant change to anything or anyone else.

In many ways it was similar to discovering that someone had cancer and then reviewing every cell in the body to find the one aberrant cell that began the chain reaction of cancer throughout the body, then, after identifying that one cell, finding a way to stop its mutation before it could affect any other cells. This must also be carried out without effecting a different mutation to other cells in the process.

It was this singularity--so difficult to isolate--that was the keystone to the program working. The real difficulty was that the singularities could in some cases be so trivial to anyone but the subject that they were extremely hard to find. Things as simple as a smile or a frown, a handshake or a head nod-- could change the course of human events. One drink too many, one compliment or even a gift given could be a rudder that steered a person's life either toward a lighthouse or toward a shipwreck.

In the case of Scott Conner the search led the team to the day of his breakdown, which was directly related to not being advanced in his job. The solution that would reset those moments leading up to the crash that sent the Madison family to George Washington Hospital was to add Conner's name to the list of people who would receive the "Golden Ticket."

Now that the singularity had been identified, the team would forward that information to Dillon Chambers so that he and Joshua Jacobs could develop an action plan for Thomas to carry out. The three-member team had worked together on over 100 cases but this was the first one that was personal, or at least the only one that they personally knew the people involved.

Chapter 43

Thomas was dressed in what he considered his normal work clothes: a tan golf shirt, blue jeans and Nike running shoes. Everything he had on was clean and neat. His shoes were simple white, designed so that someone looking at him would see him but not notice anything standing out to make them look twice.

He wore no hat, rings, or other jewelry except for a simple- looking Timex watch, but it was this simple watch that provided the ability for him to function on the team. Although the watch looked as normal as every other inexpensive watch, it was not normal at all. Enclosed within its case were additional components that possibly made it the most valuable watch on earth. Alongside of the regular mechanism was an additional set of miniature circuitry, which together with the machine allowed the wearer to be transformed and transitioned from one location to another and with the right technology from one time to another.

Dr. Reading many times had tried to explain to Thomas exactly how the process worked and Thomas tried to understand but the science was beyond his ability to conceive. So Reading shared in the simplest of terms: human beings were in essence electrical machines that functioned through electrical stimuli. The watch components charged the human body is such a way as to convert it to an electrical wave. The wave was then directed towards the machine through a cable, which then channeled the wave through the cable into a television transmission, which was then distributed through the cable system. Once the wave reached the desired location it was converted back to human form. Once the mission was completed, the process reversed itself and the subject--in this case, Thomas--was returned to the location of origination.

It was during the conversion process that the feeling of Thomas' body vibrating began and didn't completely stop until after he returned to the laboratory. This was the only part of the transition process that he didn't really enjoy.

Thomas thought back to when he first went through the complete process. He was terrified, but now his job had become very much like flying in an airplane. The frequent flyer passenger knows it is possible that something might go wrong but has arrived at the point where the fear is viewed through experience. In Thomas' experience, he had always left and returned just as he was scheduled to.

Chapter 44

Jane Bryan looked out the window of her office and thought about her involvement with Senator Madison. Her mind travelled back to their first meeting.

She was sitting alone at her favorite coffee house, straining to get the last drop of caffeine into her mouth before walking back to the counter for a refill. The place had become her favorite not because of the quality of the coffee served, although it was passable, but because of the atmosphere. She liked the quiet business of the place. She didn't like to work at home alone and the library was so clinical and quiet that the sound of the quiet seemed overwhelmingly unnatural. She needed to have a steady stream of movement and life happening around her while she wrote.

She was working on her third book. Her first foray into writing was titled *Rabbi Paul, A Study of the Life of the Apostle Paul,* which looked beyond the simplistic traditional views and more toward Paul's life as a rabbi in the center of 1st century Jewish life. Her second book *Deliverance,* about the life and history of the Jewish people as the means of world redemption, was what caught the attention of Bob Johnson, the chief of staff of Senator James Madison. This was not because Johnson was a man of faith--he wasn't--but because of the amount of detailed research into both the Bible and the many historical works used to back up her positions. Johnson was amazed by Jane's mind and thought process and how she was able to follow a spider web of seemingly unrelated pieces of a puzzle and connect them in a way that made sense. She demonstrated an ability to find things while researching that were missed by others: hidden nuggets; details in text which seemed unimportant and were easily bypassed, but when kept in the right context were not only interconnected but were required to make understanding whole. It was this ability that more often than not allowed her to find the singularities that would allow the team to change a limited event which would not impact the lives of other people and cause unintended consequences.

It was this ability that drew the attention first of Johnson and then his boss and ultimately was the reason that a senator approached a Bible student to invite her to participate in a new covert government agency. The conversation between a Bible believer, who held truth as the highest of values, and a senator, who saw truth as a commodity that rose and fell in value according to need and situation, bordered on comedy. Jane made it very clear that she would not lie nor would she even appear to bend the truth, and any request to do so would result in her immediate resignation. Though Madison had spent his entire life working with people, he had never encountered someone with such strong convictions. While he didn't agree with her beliefs, he was impressed by her commitment. With a project with as much potential for problems as the one he was forming, he felt that having someone as brilliant and committed, as Jane could be the anchor his team would need.

After establishing the groundwork of confidentiality Madison broached the topic of the morals and ethics concerning what his new team would be involved with. He was curious how Jane would respond to the idea of being able to go back and change situations in the past. He was concerned that this would conflict with her faith. Jane's answer surprised him: "I believe God is sovereign over all things, especially time, so if He provided knowledge to traverse time then no matter what we do with that knowledge, it doesn't change His sovereignty one bit."

Chapter 45

Bob Johnson felt out of sorts sitting at the head of the conference table knowing his boss the senator was in the room seated at his right hand. The six other people at the table were Thomas Green, Dillon Chambers, Jane Bryan, Yitzak Goldman, Paul West and Matthew Reading.

As this was the first time each of the people at the table had met each other, Johnson took a few moments to introduce each attendee. He also reiterated the importance of confidentiality to the success and operation of the team, and that any breach of secrecy would cause the immediate termination of the entire program. He also spelled out that although Senator Madison would head the team, he would have day-to-day operational control.

He further made plain that part of the decision to join the team was a commitment to live on the campus for at least the first year of operations. Once this meeting was adjourned, whoever chose to be a part of the team would be moved to the campus and provided with a very comfortable home with all expenses paid by the agency. This was necessary for not only the confidentiality of the program but also because so much of what they would be working on would be too time-sensitive to allow for added travel time. Any delay in their ability to assemble could cause mission failures.

It pleased Madison and Johnson that not one person hesitated to sign their contract and commit to the program.

Once the preliminary introductions and explanation of roles were carried out, Johnson began to explain what exactly the new agency would be doing. At points in his description he stopped and deferred to Madison and Dr. Reading to interject additional information and answer direct questions. It became apparent to each person assembled that this new agency would need very strict accountability to keep it from becoming the very thing the agency was being formed to stop. The inclination to use Reading's invention for personal gain would be an immense human tendency and could only be prevented by complete transparency among the team members. After all, being able to change the past could allow someone to amass great wealth, power and influence.

Johnson continued to describe the principles under which the agency would operate. He did his best to describe exactly what a transient singularity was; how they would use them to stop or reverse activities that would affect the safety of citizens of the United States; and then provided examples of how some of the actions taken by the team would be international in scope but only in as much as they affected U.S. security.

The operations flow chart would begin with Senator Madison identifying a situation that needed adjustment. He would then transmit that information to Johnson, who would direct researchers to identify the transient singularity, that fleeting moment when one item or action could be changed which would effect domino events or stop the dominos from falling so that whatever was going to happen would no longer happen.

Johnson gave an example, a traffic accident that had happened on an interstate that took the life of a congressman. This went on to cause a replacement representative being elected who would then vote against a bill necessary for security of the nation. The team would search to find how they could stop the accident from happening while simultaneously limiting the number of other events that may have been affected by the change.

In this case they would find that the person who caused the accident had stopped at a gas station to fill up his truck. While there he saw a wallet on the ground, picked it up and turned it into the employee on shift. Because he found the wallet, instead of merely paying at the pump and leaving, he entered the store and while there decided to purchase a six-pack of beer, which he started drinking on the way home. While drinking he hit a bump and spilled the beer all over. The spill distracted him and caused him to take his eyes off of the road and ultimately, to miss seeing the brake lights of the congressman's Lincoln.

His finding the wallet was the transient singularity. The way to save the congressman's life and protect the nation was to simply beat the man to discovering the wallet. This would keep him from finding the wallet, entering the store, buying the beer and killing the congressman. Simple enough.

Chapter 46

After scanning faces for almost 20 minutes Ron Blackman heard some commotion coming from the turnstile leading to the metro boarding area. From his vantage point he could only see a man in blue jeans and a t-shirt with a logo of some kind printed on the front. As he started to make his way toward the noise he watched the man walk from the turnstile towards the ticket booth.

While clearly angry, the man was not acting in a way inconsistent with any of the other metro customers who had difficulties with their pass tickets. After all, everyone was in a hurry to get somewhere and ticket problems always led to delays and even missed trains.

It wasn't until he came within 15 feet of him that he realized it was Abdul Nader walking directly towards him. What confused him was that while he had clearly identified Nader as the man he and who knows how many cops were searching for, Nader didn't seem to know he was being hunted at all. He seemed upset and frustrated but made no attempt at all to hide himself as Blackman approached. Blackman had been in law enforcement long enough to know that as long as he didn't demonstrate any actions that would seem threatening he should be able to walk right up to Abdul without causing him to become suspicious or worse yet to run. He continued to cover the last few feet between them while at the same time speaking into his microphone that he had eyes on the subject and to provide his location. Unlike a rookie, who lets the adrenaline rush cause him to start shouting into his microphone while thinking he was still whispering, Blackman calmly reported where he was and a full description of Nader to all those who had started to converge upon his position.

He arrived next to Nader just as Nader got to the ticket booth to complain that this ticket he had just purchased a few days before would not work. The metro employee took the ticket and examined it briefly before looking over at the officer who had just walked up and called him to the side of the booth. Nader could not hear what was being said between the cop and the ticket booth attendant, so he just stood there confused and tried to be patient. After a few moments Blackman asked him to step away from the booth and out of the way of the other customers. Upon being asked where he had acquired his metro ticket, Abdul responded that he had purchased it right there at that ticket booth just days before and asked why. Blackman asked Nader for identification. While Nader reached into his wallet to show him his driver's license provided for him by his trainer/handler, Blackman let him know that it appeared his metro ticket was a forgery and that he would have to wait with him while a supervisor arrived to examine the ticket.

At that moment Nader's personality and demeanor suddenly changed. Blackman could see the look in his eyes that he had seen thousands of times before: the look of an animal that has just realized it has been trapped. He could see Nader's eyes looking back and forth quickly, trying to identify a way of escape.

Nader knew that when they checked his license they would find out it was also a forgery and he would be arrested immediately. He had actually started to shift his weight to start running when he noticed how many other uniformed personnel had begun to appear and he knew that he had no way of escaping. His only hope at this point was to try and act inculpable, to let himself be arrested without resistance and then look for an opportunity to run when one presented itself.

Moments later he was handcuffed and sitting in the back seat of Blackman's car on the way to be fingerprinted and photographed.

Chapter 47

Yitzak Goldman sat across the table from Bob Johnson wondering just what he had just gotten himself into. His mind wandered back to the last time he felt as challenged as he did now. It was the earlier challenge that ignited his interest in chemistry and eventually brought him to get his degree in chemical engineering. It was also the thing that drew him away from his Jewish upbringing.

He was in his grandfather's house studying the Talmud when his uncle asked him a question about the text, challenging him to prove the text was correct. To this day Yitzak doesn't think his uncle thought he would accept the challenge. But he did-- and the end result of his research and study was that he realized it was un-provable.

This conclusion caused Yitzak to begin to doubt his faith altogether because anything that wasn't provable could not be real. From that point on he spent his time in science, breaking the hearts of his family as he first drifted and then completely walked away from Judaism.

His studies brought him to the consistency of chemicals, and their proper mixing so they would do what they were supposed to. Each and every time you knew what you started with and you knew what you would end up with. Chemistry was solid. Knowing this allowed him to put his trust in something he felt was real.

Science followed rules. Theories made sense--they were either provable or they were false. Science had laws like gravity, thermodynamics, laws of motion. Each was provable in a laboratory or at least by theory.

To Yitzak all of these things made sense and allowed his mind to be settled in ways that faith did not. Faith required ... well, faith. It was only provable to the point that it was accepted, but ultimately at some point one had to take a step of faith. It was this step that Yitzak was so opposed to. He just could not bring himself to walk over that edge and hope that God was standing there to catch him.

Everything in his life had become solid and fit neatly into his scientific box. That is, until he met Bob Johnson and Matthew Reading. Reading's invention somehow violated many of the laws he had come to trust and believe in. Without warning he had encountered something that caused him to be provoked in a way he had not experienced since he was a child. The rug had been pulled out from under his feet and with it the very ground the rug had rested upon was no longer there.

For the second time in his life Yitzak was having a crisis of faith, only this time it wasn't about religion but science. His world had shifted until he found himself looking for a new foundation to stand upon.

Chapter 48

Senator Madison made his way into the hospital after his meeting with the team. Thankfully the hospital was able to move both children into the same room after surgery. Now he was sitting there trying to keep his eyes on both of his children at the same time. The pediatric ICU was different from the sterile-looking environment of the adult version. While there were the same IV stands, blood pressure units and oxygen pumps, they also had bright colors and upbeat-looking paintings on the walls. But it was still hard for any parent to be looking down at their little ones lying in beds, immobilized by restraints, with wires and tubes sticking out of their bodies.

Both James Jr. and Annabel had made it through the extensive procedures and now it was simply time to wait and see how their little bodies responded to the surgery and drug therapy.

Madison had already spent time with his wife in her room and now was in a daze as he watched his children's chests rise and fall with every struggled breath. Even more difficult was the internal struggle he was enduring from knowing that although his wife and children were just grasping onto life at this moment, he had set in motion a plan that, if successful, would make everything happening right now moot.

As he looked into the faces of his children, he knew what they were going through physically and mentally. Their pain was obvious, it was so severe that it was noticeable even through the medication. How could he express sincere compassion while knowing that if all went well, neither his wife, children nor anyone else including himself would even have withstood the accident and hospital treatment?

He was bearing something that to his knowledge no one had ever gone through before. He may have been the first person to know that his personal history was about to change. Everything that had taken place over the past few days would no longer exist: not the accident, the phone calls, and the surgeries. He wondered to himself, what would it be like? Would there be a moment that he realized that time had shifted? Would there be a flash of light or a sudden feeling that something was happening without knowing what it was? Would it be what people refer to as déjà-vu, a feeling that you had lived through something before? He knew that his family would not have any memories about the time shift. But with his knowledge of the program and the machine, and with his foreknowledge that they were going to change the course of events, would he know?

He was having a very difficult time differentiating between his emotions, racked as they were by the sight of his babies in pain versus his rational knowledge that their pain was only real right now. But once the mission was successful they would never have actually been in pain at all.

After sitting a while longer and hoping one of them would open their eyes, he made a stop by Anne's room to check on her before heading back to the office. Just as he arrived there a team of doctors entered whispering to one another in that annoying way doctors do: loud enough for you to know they are talking about your case but too softly for you to understand what they are saying. In the lead was Chief Surgeon Dr. Ray Attila, who walked directly up to Madison while introducing himself and his team and speaking in the most serious of voices to explain the conditions of Anne, James Jr. and Annabel. "They are all very critical having suffered severe trauma. In all honesty the damage was so massive that unless a miracle happens it is doubtful that they will survive," he said.

Dr. Attila was used to the whole spectrum of reactions from his patients' families, but he was somewhat befuddled when the senator simply said, "Thank you for all you have done," turned and walked out the door.

Chapter 49

Hakim Aziz was standing outside his home in hopes that a breeze would blow by bringing a momentary cooling in the midst of the evening heat. He had been in this same spot for over two hours now while awaiting a phone call from America.

He had worked out every detail, studied every possible problem, and had conceived of what he considered a perfect plan. They had found and trained Abdul Nader and conditions had exceeded expectations as each stage of the mission took shape. Nader had completed his training ahead of schedule and excelled in learning both English and Spanish. The Spanish was harder because he needed to overcome his Iraqi accent while speaking it, where with English there were so many Americans from the Middle East that an Iraqi speaking without an accent would have stood out more than if he spoke the broken English of an immigrant.

Nader had never been late checking in before and this concerned Hakim, who had many things he needed to do but didn't want to move away from the phone and miss Nader's call. He had spoken to Nader the day before to brief him one last time and to walk through the mission step- by-step. After all, everything he had trained Nader for would depend on each step of the plan being followed through on exactly.

Nader had gone over the plan vocally three times the night before without missing a beat, from when he would get up to where he would buy his coffee to how he would purchase his metro ticket and exactly how to carry his backpack.

Hakim was confident after the phone call that Nader would complete his mission and return the next day to Iraq to return to his normal life, content to be a hero in secret.

So when Nader missed his scheduled contact time, Hakim was surprised. Now that two hours had elapsed from the appointed time, he had shifted from surprise to concern and had begun to pace back and forth. The path he was making into the dirt had become a small trench.

Finally after almost three hours the phone rang and startled Hakim, who had focused so much on waiting for the phone to ring that when it did he jumped.

It was not Nader on the line; instead it was Hakim's older brother Abrahim whose excited tone made it clear immediately that something was wrong. He told Hakim to turn on the news pronto. While Hakim did so Abrahim continued to inform him of what had taken place: Nader had been arrested, the attack had not happened. He was not sure how it transpired but all he knew was that Nader was arrested for having a counterfeit Metro ticket.

This new information made Hakim's mind spin. He attempted to separate the information into details he could understand and then endeavored to deal with them one at a time. He began to ask himself questions. Where was Adbul? How did he get a fake Metro ticket? Would Abdul break when questioned?

Beyond a shadow of a doubt, he believed that once he knew all the facts of what had happened; he would be able to come up with a reasoned response. Inside his head he said, "This is bad, but not beyond fixing somehow."

However, the next words he heard shook him to his core. Abrahim said in a low but clear voice, "Hakim, you have failed us, come immediately to my house."

It wasn't until just that moment that he understood just how bad things were.

Chapter 50

Dr. Paul West's involvement with the team was the aftermath of a lecture that Bob Johnson attended with his wife. Bob didn't really want to go. As a matter of fact, when his wife told him they would be attending he tried to think of any possible excuse to bow out. There were few things Bob liked less than attending a lecture with people who thought they were so far above everyone else that their feet never touched the ground when they walked. Add that level of overwhelming snobbery to a lecture on classical music and Bob would have much rather had his teeth drilled for two hours non-stop than be in that audience. But Bob loved his wife and was willing to take this bullet to make her happy. He mumbled under his breath "Happy wife, happy life," and growled just a bit.

The lecture was not at all what Bob had expected. Somehow Paul West managed to make classical music not only interesting but also relevant to Bob in a way that no one else had ever done. West was able to speak of music not just in terms of notes, melodies and rhythms; he was also able to weave the musical scores into patterns that made sense. The pattern and connection of sounds had never been expressed in a way that brought them beyond a music sheet or a dry symphony into an almost visible image projected upon the listeners' closed eyelids. This perceived image was produced, by a blending of each instrument together as an artist blends colors to turn unrelated blotches on canvas into a masterpiece.

What really caught Johnson's attention was the way Dr. West was not only competent to speak about the interconnection of each note but was able to present those connections in a way that made sense even to someone like Bob, who had come into the room with absolutely no desire to enjoy the talk.

Bob's amazement resulted in his investigating the life and history of Dr. Paul West. After receiving the background information an invitation was sent for a face-to-face chat, which ultimately resulted in an invitation to the gathering and an offer to join the team.

Turned out as he always was, Dr. West entered that meeting looking every bit the educational elitist nerd: blue slacks neatly pressed with sharp creases; white button-down shirt with a red bow tie; and a corduroy blazer complete with leather elbow pads. West regularly wore a bow tie; the color or pattern may have varied but a bow tie it always was.

Dr. West was the third member of the triumvirate jokingly called the Justice League after the children's cartoon they had all grown up watching. Although the three of them were the type of people always chosen last for a sports team and they would never have been considered superheroes, they would soon have the power to effectuate change that could save the world.

When Bob Johnson first provided these three names and their bios to Senator Madison, the senator nearly choked on his coffee. But as Johnson undertook to explain, each team member's, unique qualifications, Madison warmed to the idea a little, though he withheld his endorsement until he saw what they could do. His last words were, "Well, if they fail too badly we can always go back in time and fix it." He was only half-joking.

Chapter 51

Abrahim opened the door for his brother before he even knocked. He had been waiting on his arrival, hoping for some explanation of what had happened in America. How could things have gone so wrong when they had worked out every detail and gone over each action until Abdul could walk the plan through without a single deviation? All Abrahim knew was that he and his brother were in trouble. No --trouble was too mild a term. They needed to find out what had gone wrong and how to repair the damage done before anyone else caught on about it. Even now they were on borrowed time as it would only be a matter of time until someone else would see the news and put two and two together and start looking for them.

After all, the whole concept of this attack was theirs. They conceived it, chose the participants, provided the training and set everything in motion. If their plan had been successful they would have been recognized as heroes. However, as it now stood they would be mocked as embarrassing failures and their associates tainted. Hakim had handled training and operation logistics but Abrahim had made the connections and arranged for financing. He boldly promised and committed to some very powerful men. Now he could hardly breathe because of the overpowering fear that gripped him. He rushed Hakim into the house trying to formulate all of the questions he wanted to ask. All the what's, why's, where's and how's swirled around like sand in a sand storm. He wanted to speak but could not focus his mind enough to formulate a rational phrase; all that came out of his mouth was a bungled garbled mix of growl and grunt.

The two men eyed each other and saw in each other's eyes the same thing: terror of what was about to happen to them. Hakim stared at his brother as a younger brother reaches out to an older brother for safety, all the while knowing that this time there would be no protection possible.

Once their sponsors found out that they had not achieved the event they had promised, their lives would be ended. They would pray for a swift death,

but they knew it would not come. Their punishment
would be held up as an example to all who followed.

Chapter 52

Thomas woke up and sat up in one complete movement. He knew that most people woke up by just opening their eyes and looking around. Some only opened their eyes for a moment and would roll over to go back to sleep, trying to regain that almost unreachable state of total peace found when sleeping soundly. But for Thomas, for as far back as he could remember, the moment his eyes opened he also sat straight up in bed, ready to begin whatever the day had for him.

This morning, as with every morning since he had begun working in the program, he was not sure what he would be doing or where he would be going. But he knew that whatever it was he would be assigned to, somehow it would be saving lives or preventing catastrophes.

Although Thomas always knew what he was doing and what his mission was, he was never privy to what the outcome of his mission would be. He knew that he was to move one item; add a name to a list;

speak a sentence in a meeting; or direct someone down one road instead of the other. He also knew that by doing these things he would be changing outcomes that would redirect events to prevent tragedies. However, as part of program policies, he was never told what event he was trying to either prevent or bring about.

Madison and Johnson knew that if Thomas knew what the event was he might decide to help out in some way that would adversely affect the desired outcome. So before Thomas started his morning exercise ritual, he watched the news and read online news sites, each day trying to figure out which events might have resulted from his missions.

This was very difficult to know because he worked to bring things about in such a way that no one else would know anything had changed. So Thomas would watch the news and see an election result and wonder, did I cause that? He would hear the announcement of a power couple's marriage and wonder if his work had brought the people together.

He would see businesses merge and wonder about the merger, "Did I do that?"

He knew he could not have been responsible for all the things that went on every day that impacted thousands if not millions of lives, but it was fun for him to daydream a little and consider the possibilities. If he couldn't really know what he had accomplished at least he could revel in the prospects.

Then Thomas put down his computer, turned off the television and got up out of bed. As always he dressed in simple workout clothes depending on the weather: either shorts, which he preferred, or a workout suit during the colder months. After doing whatever workout routine he was assigned for the morning, he would walk to the office where he would be provided appropriate garments for his first mission of the day.

The clothes he wore totally depended on where he was going and what he was going to do. Choosing clothing for normal people only required knowing the dress code: casual; business casual; formal or maybe even black tie. But for Thomas, the question of era had to be figured into his wardrobe decisions. Every year required adjustments that went from miniscule changes all the way to a major style shift. While considering the styles required for each assignment, Thomas' handlers also had to consider that whatever he wore was supposed to fit in such a way that no one would take notice.

So Thomas went to the showers and emerged looking every bit as if he stepped out of 2000.

Chapter 53

The youngest and newest member of the senator's team, 24-year old Michelle Gregg, brought a special background in television that allowed her to contribute in a very exceptional way to the team's accomplishments. She didn't labor behind or in front of the camera, but spent her days scheduling the various programs and interspersing the commercials at their appropriate times. She was a unique person who had a gift for organization and didn't mind being in small room in front of a computer screen for hours at a time. She needed almost no social interaction to be content though she wasn't anti-social and when necessary, had no problem at all being part of a crowd.

It was a matter of conversation among the team members because Michelle had youth, looks and intelligence going for her and yet she chose to spend her time sitting at her desk searching the web for information. Unlike many of her peers in this age of computer technology, social media sites were of no interest to her. She really didn't care who was trending at any given time because trends were of no interest to her at all.

The team had progressed and completed many missions since its formation. However, after working through the details of over 20 such operations, Johnson and Chambers determined that they needed a specialist in the functioning of television programming and scheduling. After advertising for candidates through traditional job search websites they finally concluded that Michelle was the only truly qualified candidate.

Michelle's role on the team was to use the information provided about the transient singularity provided by West, Bryan and Goldman, and then search through television programming to find the best insertion and recall time for the mission. This required more than just a simple knowledge of what was on television at any given time. It also required an in-depth knowledge of the way programming was laid out between commercials and episodes. Michelle had to know the program details so that she knew when and where Thomas would be inserted so the timing of his actions could be planned and the timing for his recall could also be planned, each which required exact timing down to seconds. Michelle knew what programs were most helpful. The program featuring police agencies proved very valuable to her because most were set in major cities where the majority of the movers, shakers and power brokers lived and worked. They provided steady locations such as courthouses and police departments, which always were available, and also a variety of locales such as hotels, neighborhoods, schools and stores depending on the different episodes. Once an insertion program was chosen then Michelle had to work out the timing for Thomas' travel and completion of his task. She also had to provide a pathway for Thomas to return to the current time to the campus. This tended to be the more difficult portion of her job.

For some missions this could be accomplished simply by using the different seasons of a long-running program. An older season may be running on one network, while the current season was airing on a different network, which allowed for Thomas to travel to and from a single location during different time periods.

When using different seasons of a single program wasn't possible, Michelle used the network newly formed by the agency to provide a combination of vintage programming and commercials as well as modern programs and commercials to make available transition points from present to past and back.

Once Michelle formulated the transportation itinerary down to the second, this information was passed on to Johnson, who would then have Thomas' watch programmed with the time coordinates.

Chapter 54

Working in the mailroom of a large multi-national corporation had almost no perks of any kind. Everyone who worked there did so in hopes it would be the proverbial foot in the door that opened the way to a job upstairs doing something more important, or at least a job viewed as more important by those who got their mail from the very same people considered so unimportant. Every day like ants skittering from floor to floor delivering contracts, invoices, and millions of dollars in checks from clients and future clients, the mail attendants walked who knows how many miles throughout the building, pushing their carts and dropping off all of the correspondence that made the big wigs upstairs rich.

Yet there was one day every year those working in the mailroom looked forward to, to the point that they actually ran a lottery to choose who would be the one to deliver the invitations to the yearly conference. They didn't look forward to this because any of them mistakenly believed that he or she might be invited. No, they wanted to deliver the envelopes so they could watch those waiting so impatiently, see if they had been chosen. While this was the one-day when the mailroom became important, it was also the one-day that people who worked "upstairs" found out that most of them were also considered unimportant.

This year's lottery winner was Bill, a short heavyset man in his thirties who accepted the mailroom job when he was 24, knowing that it would only be a short-term job until he could make his way upstairs to a better job in one of the many cubicles with limited walking required.

He gathered up the invitation letters and looked at the lists, then double-checked the number of names on the list against the number of invitation envelopes. He counted twice and then again a third time. In the past there were always 50 invitations. This year the list had 51 and the envelopes were 51. The numbers matched but it didn't make sense. He thought to himself, "Hmmm, this doesn't make sense. Well, who cares? No one upstairs makes sense; if they did, I would not still be pushing a mail cart."

He arrived on the floor to deliver the invitations and exited the elevator. Everyone on the floor knew what was on his cart and each one did his or her best to watch him walk down the aisle without appearing interested in the least. The looks on their faces almost made working the rest of the year in the mailroom worth it.

He took his time walking, stretching each moment out. With each step he passed another row of cubicle desks and as if each head were programmed to follow his movements like a security camera, heads swiveled almost in one fluid motion. He stopped for a moment to tie his shoe, which really didn't need to be tied, but it gave him that much longer to enjoy his victory. After all, times like this did not come but once a year. He stopped again to pick up a piece of paper on the floor, something he would have never done any other day, but today time was important, so the longer this took the better. As he continued down the pathway between the rows, he could see desperation on many faces. The same people that walked around the rest of the year as if they owned the world, for these few moments, were his to toy with.

He had taken as long as he could without it being so obvious that he would receive complaints from his boss in the mailroom, so he made it to the mailbox. Each person had his own little cubbyhole; since there were hundreds of people working on this floor, there was a corresponding number of cubbyholes. This allowed Bill to take even more time to look at each envelope individually, check the name and the box number, and then gingerly insert the invitation into the box. After what seemed to all those watching an extraordinary amount of time to deliver 50 envelopes, Bill completed his gig and began to make his way back to the elevator. He walked just as slowly on his return trip for two reasons. First, he didn't want it to be too obvious that he had purposely taken his time and also, because he wanted to be there to see the demonstrations of those who received the invitations and those who did not.

The 51st envelope had been delivered to the box of Scott Conner.

Chapter 55

Anne Madison gathered up her children from the playground swings and started to make her way back to the minivan. She looked at James and Annabel and was amazed at how they could both have spent three hours playing in a park. While James was covered from head to toe with dirt and grime, Annabel was somehow pristine from crown to slipper. They were in the same place for the same amount of time and for all intents and purposes did the exact same things, though her son was going to wear much of the park's dirt home with him while her daughter could nearly sit down for high tea without anyone knowing what she had done all afternoon.

She herded them toward the car in a way only a mother can. All the way to the car James complained about having to go home and couldn't he just stay a little while longer, while Annabel did her best to galvanize her mother to make sure she was home in time to watch her favorite television program. Anne went through the same level of struggle getting James into the seat and seat belt as she had before the trip to the park began. She finally succeeded and buckled them back into their car seats to prepare for the trip home.

She looked at her clock on the dashboard and knew that if all went well, it would only be another hour before her husband was home. Then the changing of the guards would occur and she would have a bit of time to herself while he played with the children and went through his regular evening routine, which included baths and a story before both parents tucked the children into bed for the night.

While the traffic to the park was light and swifter moving than normal, the ride home was just the opposite. There seemed to be either roadwork or a disabled vehicle from the start of the drive until the end. The children were relatively quiet except for when their video ended, and a battle commenced between James who wanted to watch the same video again and Annabel who wanted a different one.

Because of the extra length of the trip she actually arrived home just after James who had already made his way into the house. When he heard the garage door opening James walked out to assist with unloading the children out of the van. This moment was what he looked forward to all day. He loved to spend time with his children. He loved to crawl and roll on the ground and he loved to watch their eyes as they experienced new things.

He carried James, who had used up all of his energy fighting against being entrapped in his seatbelt and arguing with his sister about the video. While he carried James he held Annabel's hand. They walked into the house and he watched as his wife quietly walked toward the peace of her bedroom. He knew she would be lowering herself into a bathtub and that he would not see or hear from her for at least an hour.

James gathered the two children into the kitchen and warmed up their dinner, which had been prepared earlier and placed in the refrigerator by

Anne. He took a moment to marvel at how such a simple meal brought such joy to his children.

After the meal was complete and while Anne was in her bath, he took James to have his bath while Annabel watched her daily episode of whatever princess was being featured. After finishing James' bath the children switched places and Annabel bathed while James half-watched, half-slept through a cartoon about a train.

After bath times for all were completed, Anne and James tucked their children into bed for the night. After reading a story to them, James did something he had never done before: he knelt between their beds and uttered a short prayer, then leaned over and kissed both children on the head.

Chapter 56

Thomas stood quietly in the closet waiting until the time for him to exit would come. He felt the familiar vibration of his watch and walked out into the living room, down the hallway and out the side door of the home. He stuck the small tab in between the lock and the doorjamb and quickly walked down the street almost a quarter mile. He had only 25 minutes to finish his task and return to the house to be transported back home.

As he walked across the road he picked up a shiny red ball and carried it with him, placing it carefully in the yard just across from where he had found it when he arrived. He turned and walked back in the direction that he had come from when he realized that something about this place seemed very familiar. Because he never knew the details of any of his missions he had no idea what event would be changed by moving an inexpensive shiny red plastic ball from one side of the road to the other. He just knew that whatever would be changed was significant enough to require the intervention of his agency.

He continued to walk with that strange déjà-vu feeling in his mind. He looked back one more time to make sure no one had noticed him and that the ball was still where it was supposed to be when he noticed two things and immediately realized why he felt as if he had been here before. Just up the road he saw a small boy riding his tricycle across the street trying to get to his shiny red ball, and he also saw a car driving directly at the child when suddenly a very average-looking Honda veered right into the path of the car, crashing into the oncoming vehicle and saving the child's life.

About the Author

Rabbi Eric Tokajer is a husband, father and grandfather. He is the Rabbi at Brit Ahm Messianic Synagogue in Pensacola, Florida. He also is the Publisher and Executive Director of the Messianic Times Newspaper. In addition to these two roles, he also serves as the Theology Team Facilitator for the TLV Family Bible Project. He is a sought after speaker for both national and international conferences and events. For more information about Rabbi Eric, visit www.RabbiEricT.com.

www.ingramcontent.com/pod-product-compliance
Lightning Source LLC
Chambersburg PA
CBHW070120260626
47160CB00004B/1546